WHO ATE THE AVOCADOS?

TIME TO LAUGH ABOUT DIVORCE

ROSE AJAR

This is a work of fiction. Names, characters, places, and incidents either are the products of the author's imagination or are used fictitiously. Similarities to actual persons, living or dead, business establishments, events or locales is entirely coincidental.

For more information, visit the author's website at roseajar.com

Who Ate the Avocados? – First Edition
ISBN: 979-8-9917397-0-2 (ebook)
ISBN: 979-8-9917397-1-9 (trade paperback)
First published in the United States in 2025

CONTENTS

Introduction

ACT ONE: SPLITTING UP: CASH, PEANUTS, AND COMPLICATIONS

I WILL ALWAYS BE THERE TO PAY FOR YOUR PHONE BILL

IT IS PEANUTS

THE MUSICAL CHAIRS

ACT TWO: LET'S GO GROCERY SHOPPING!

WHO ATE THE AVOCADOS?

TOMATO TOM-AH-TO

TEAM BREAD VERSUS TEAM CEREALS

SISYPHUS, OR THE MYTH OF GROCERY SHOPPING

FINALLY, A LITTLE BIT OF ART

ACT THREE: RUN, RUN, RUN!

EPILOGUE: THE RISE OF THE DOLPHIN

GET READY, GIRL!

DIVORCE DAY, PART ONE

THE COUCH, OR JUST HALF OF IT

THE TOILET PAPER HEIST

WHEN JOHN REALIZED HIS TOILET PAPER WAS GONE

DIVORCE DAY, PART TWO

CURTAIN CALL

#MASHTHEAVOCADO

To my grandmother, a dedicated teacher who instilled in me a love for beautiful words from an early age. Your love, affection and sharp wit have shaped me into the woman I am today.

To my grandfather as well, whose boundless love and unwavering pride will forever uplift me.

To my two children: You are the loves and lights of my life.

To my dear friend and Editor, Arielle, who gave me the greatest gift of all: Your feedback, sharp edits and fresh perspectives, which added the perfect flavor to this book.

Introduction

This is the fictional tale of John and Jane, two ordinary people navigating the extraordinary minefield of divorce. Like many other couples, they can't seem to agree on anything—not groceries, not furniture, certainly not who ate the last avocado. And why settle their differences quietly when you can take your show to court?

But here is the twist: Until their court date arrives, John, Jane, and their two children must continue living under the same roof, as no custody arrangement for their children is in place. This domestic comedy unfolds in the most uncomfortable waiting room imaginable: their shared apartment.

As our story opens, they stand at the mailbox, awaiting the court letter that will tell them how long this unique form of domestic purgatory will last. How many months before they can face the judge who will finally untangle the knot they tied seven years ago?

One crisp January morning, a letter arrived from the court. John spotted it first, tucked between a grocery store coupon and a pizza flyer. The envelope sat there, innocent as a tomato in summer, containing news that would shape the next chapter of their unraveling story.

Jane found John in the kitchen, reading the letter over and over, his face growing paler by the second. July fifth. The court date for their divorce was set for July fifth. The horror of this revelation crashed over them in waves. As reality sank in, their thoughts spiraled:

Jane: Six months . . . of awkward silences in the hallway.

John: Six months . . . of reorganizing the kitchen cupboards at midnight.

Jane: Six months . . . of cooking salmon at 6 AM just because I can.

John: Six months . . . of extremely well-timed shower occupancy.

Jane: Six months . . . of Netflix asking "Are you still watching?"

John: Six months . . . of racing to get the mail first.

And then, in a rare moment of synchronicity, they both had the exact same thought:

Six months . . . Together . . . How could we . . . ?

Six months of fighting over the thermostat settings. Six months of passive-aggressive dish stacking. Six months of treating leftovers like state secrets. Like characters in a comedy they never auditioned for, they would be required to continue their domestic dance for half a year, sharing the same space, breathing the same air, arguing over the same avocados.

That evening, John paced the master bedroom, muttering the contents of the court letter while recording himself on his phone. He'd play it back anytime he was unsure about the exact details of the meeting, *Court date: July fifth. Time: 9:30 a.m. Location: second floor, room 201.* He was reviewing his eleventh recording when he heard Jane moving around restlessly in the living room. Down the hall, Jane was marking big red Xs on her calendar, counting down the days until July. She color-coded the full calendar, but the date remained stubbornly fixed in July.

They were trapped. Together. For Six Months. Until Court Do Them Part.

In those six months still living together, they will bicker over every little detail of daily life. But settle out of court? Not a chance.

Imagine a novel that takes all the futile conflicts with your ex, all those leftover scraps of arguments, and turns them into a garden of entertainment.

Imagine a novel that spins the absurdity of it all into hilarious tales.

Buckle up for a refreshing ride through the absurdities of someone else's divorce.

ACT ONE

SPLITTING UP: CASH, PEANUTS, AND COMPLICATIONS

I will always be there to pay for your phone bill

The January morning after the court letter arrived, Jane woke up feeling like a powerhouse. After a few stretches and push-ups, she was ready to get to the task: moving her single mattress from the master bedroom of their family apartment to the living room. All by herself. Such a strong, independent woman ready to take on the world.

Their marital bed mirrored perfectly their relationship: mismatched, odd, and already split in two. A year ago, Jane and John went on a mission to replace their worn-out queen-sized mattress, which sagged in the middle and had uneven slopes. Jane wanted medium-firm while John wanted extra-firm. Our two married strangers landed on a compromise: buying one metallic bed frame but two separate mattresses to fit their irreconcilable tastes. Little did Jane know that this would greatly simplify her decision to move her sleeping quarters to the living room a year later. With a deep breath, she grabbed hold of her medium-firm mattress and began her Herculean task of pushing it through the apartment's narrow hallway. The mattress seemed to resist at first. Sweat formed on her forehead as she pushed, each shove feeling like pushing away years of trying to make it work.

She kept pushing forward. It was hard work, but she was undeterred. She would get to the end of this. She would get to the end of the hallway. After what felt like an eternity of pushing and adjusting angles, Jane triumphantly rolled her wrinkled but victorious mattress into the living room (the room which would become her semi-private space for the months to come, to the great dismay and horror of her soon-to-be ex-husband John). Next job on the list: relocating her chest of drawers. She was a pro now.

She looked around the remodeled living room, a small smile playing on her lips. The transformation was complete. Her mattress now dominated the once-bare floor. Framed photographs she'd kept in drawers were now proudly displayed on shelves. Charging cables danced across furniture that had never known such chaos.

Four months ago, Jane told John she wanted a divorce. Their marriage had been strained for years, with both feeling unhappy long before she finally decided to speak up. They initially turned to mediation in hopes of resolving things outside of court, but the process quickly broke down. When their discussions fell apart and no resolution was in sight, it became clear that only a judge could untangle the knot. With tension rising, the idea of sharing a bedroom with someone she would soon face in court? Not a chance.

She collapsed on her mattress, which rested softly on the floor of the living room. Every muscle in her body ached from the effort, but her spirit felt lighter than it had in months. She felt exhausted and victorious, knowing that from now on, her bedroom would be wherever she decided it should be. Her next move would be to get out of this apartment entirely. One step at a time.

The sound of keys in the lock announced John's return from work. The front door swung open, revealing John frozen in the doorway, his briefcase dangling from suddenly limp fingers as he took in the transformed living room. He felt as if he had just walked into an alternate reality, and it took a moment for his mind to catch up: Jane's mattress and chest of drawers had taken up residence in his living room. What the hell?

John could not move.

John could not look away.

John was trapped in this bizarre scene where Jane's material possessions were taking over: The lonely mattress humbly placed on the floor seemed to be mocking him and the sturdy and durable chest of drawers placed next to it was amplifying the mockery. Jane's furniture was obviously conspiring against him, judging him, side-eying him, questioning what he did or did not do, what he said or did not say over the past few years.

John's moment of self-reflection and introspection was short-lived. More distressing and urgent thoughts began to fill his mind. The truth struck him like a banana landing on racers in Mario Kart: His wife had conquered the living room.

On this dreadful day, she had planted her flag, her pillow, and her pajamas.

She had indicated a few months prior that she was leaving him, but it turned out she did not leave at all, she just started the siege of the living room! He looked again at her furniture, angry this time. The mattress and drawers were still chuckling at his disarray, whispering secrets of this new living arrangement he did not understand and agree to.

After the disgust and the anger caused by this act of war, came the worry. If she did this to his living room, she was capable of anything. What had she done to his bed? He dashed to the master bedroom, ready for disaster. But no, he breathed a sigh of relief, the king-size metallic bed frame was still there, but now it proudly supported just one mattress, his prized extra-firm one, instead of the two single mattresses that used to coexist in uneasy harmony. Not the type of bedroom décor you would post on Instagram, but at least his stuff was untouched. He immediately found himself straightening the edges of his solo mattress which had been slightly displaced during Jane's expedition. As if perfect alignment could somehow fix what was broken.

Then, returning to the living room, he surveyed the scene with the precision of an architect. He was now devastated. Jane's mattress and drawers occupied exactly two-thirds of the living room. Two-thirds. That was more than half. It was nighttime, the children were already in bed, and there she was, comfortably sitting on the couch she had moved to the other side of the living room to make room for her stuff. She had her back turned to him, but he could tell she was smiling. She was internally celebrating her victory. What a masterpiece she had just pulled off right under his nose. He had been caught off guard, but he would not let it happen again. Now was the time to confront her.

John took a deep breath.

John: Can you please explain what you did just here?

Jane responded, spinning some tale about how separated people usually decide to sleep in separate beds and separate rooms. Yeah, right. Her bad faith was reaching a new high, she just wanted to annex the living room. He told her so.

Jane sighed.

Jane: I see you have deep concerns here and will try to alleviate some of them. Why don't we alternate every month who gets the right to annex the living room?

This was a serious topic, and she was being funny again. Of course he would never entertain sleeping in the living room. A living room is not a sleeping area. She continued rambling and concluded saying that she thus did not have a choice but stay in the living room until their court hearing. The much-anticipated hearing that would finally allow them to physically separate by establishing a parenting schedule for their two children, Milo and Mia. Wrong. In life, one always has a choice. And John? He had never pushed her out. Annexing the living room was her own decision.

John reflected on this unilateral decision Jane just made. She would occupy two thirds of the living room for the next six months. Would he be able to live in such poor living conditions that long?

After a moment of strained silence, Jane decided to expand the conversation and address some other topics regarding their separated life under the same roof.

Jane, careful but determined: While we're establishing new boundaries, I think we should discuss our financial arrangements too. The bank account, the bills, all of it.

John's expression tightened. First the living room, now their finances? But before he could protest, Jane continued and shifted into the practical tone she'd perfected during their marriage.

Jane: Our shared bank account is almost empty. I think we should stop using it. We can take turns shopping for the house each week and settle the difference at the end of each month. For everything else not related to the kids or home, we'll pay separately. How does that sound?

Her voice remained steady, but beneath that practiced calm, her heart raced. Each word felt like laying another brick in the wall between them. As she spoke, she watched John's expression harden, that familiar look of resistance spreading across his face. She braced herself for the objection she knew was coming. Of course, John would argue. Jane was systematically dismantling their shared life piece by piece. Panic rose in his chest. Why was she rushing everything? He needed to slow this down, to keep things as they were until he decided they were ready to change. This was all moving too fast, in directions he neither understood nor approved.

John: Slow down. You are flooding me with information. We are still married, we have not agreed on anything as it relates to our separation, so why change anything? We have always shared expenses; I see no reason to stop now.

Although John made it clear that he wanted the discussion to end, Jane pressed on, providing practical examples.

Jane: Look, it's simple. I buy my own lunches at work. You buy yours. I pay for my haircuts, you pay for yours. Same for dinners with friends, nail salons, personal phone bills . . .

John: You don't understand the principle. Technically, we're still married.

Jane: Yes, but I'm not going to make you pay for my gym membership. Which, let's be honest, is a complete waste of money since I never actually go. We shouldn't be paying for each other's personal stuff anymore. Just split the things we both need—you know, for the house and the kids.

John was outraged. Once again, she was only looking out for herself, driven by selfish motives. But he was not about to let her have her way. She already had deprived him of his living-room space. She would not deprive him of the comfort of sharing all his life's expenses with her. She was still his wife, after all. It was getting late, yet the moon seemed to whisper encouragement in his ear and was casting its bright light on him. John would stand firm, he would not back down.

John: Then the mobile phone bill is a household expense. I absolutely need it, not just for me, but also for the sake of our children.

Jane: But that's . . .

John: The only reason why you don't want to count it as a shared expense is because your employer pays for it, while mine does not. So, my phone bill should be a shared expense.

Jane frowned, struggling to repress a big laugh. Should she be contributing to her ex's phone bill until Death Do Them Part? Was that what modern-life divorce was like? Should they also be sharing phone records? She pinched herself to maintain composure as she restrained herself from blurting out a good joke. She imagined saying: *Well, you see, I have been thinking. Since you do not answer my messages when I ask for your input for anything kids-related, and since you dodge my calls when you are alone with the kids, why should I foot the bill for your mobile phone? It's like paying for a service I am not really receiving, right?*

John did not understand why Jane was smiling. Was she preparing another ambush? The living room, his phone, and then what? What else could she take away from him?

John's Journal: "180 days until the court hearing . . . Filing emergency motion against phone plan separation. What's next—separate Netflix accounts?"

Jane's Journal: "180 days until the court hearing . . . Phone plan seeking divorce on grounds of cellular incompatibility. Netflix profile already in witness protection. Amazon Prime considering filing for sole custody of the shipping benefits."

It is peanuts

John and Jane had evolved into amateur philosophers, debating their own existential question: To share, or not to share an expense? That was the question. Their solution? Monthly receipt exchanges that turned their dining table into a courtroom where even a loaf of bread could stand trial. For these two, receipt-trading had become a bizarre ritual, the last thing they still shared besides an address and two kids.

On this Saturday night in early February, John began his review of Jane's January receipts. These small papers were his last connection to his wife's daily life—proof that she still existed in his ordered world. He convinced himself this was just normal budget tracking. With the fervor of an archaeologist uncovering ancient secrets, John scrutinized the numbers, items, dates, and locations, looking for suspicious activities over the past month. His dedication finally paid off when he spotted an anomaly.

John: Jane, I need to talk to you.

Jane: Now? I was about to go to bed.

John: This is important. I think you will want to hear this.

Jane: All right. I am listening.

John: I was going through the receipts and saw you've slipped in one hundred and forty-two dollars for your personal Amazon Prime annual membership under our shared expenses. Really? That's a personal expense, not a shared one! You were all about excluding my phone bill, even though I use it for parenting, which, you know, is kind of important. How about you take that Amazon charge out and keep things a bit more reasonable?

Jane: That membership is for the whole family to get our packages faster. It's quite different from a phone, which you are the only one to use. But no problem, I'll remove it from the total and pay for all of it myself.

John: There is more.

At the start of the conversation, Jane was tired; now, she was intrigued. John was exulting. What had he discovered in her receipts? This was real life, not a well-crafted telenovela. If it had been, this instant would have been the best time to launch the commercials. Jane could not deal with the tension anymore. She had to know.

John could feel that she was burning to hear his words. The air was heavy and electric. John savored the silence like a forbidden fruit.

The silence dragged on. Jane knew what John was doing and she started turning around, slowly, hoping for him to start talking.

John watched Jane turning around. He was satisfied. She was ready to retreat. He could now express himself with confidence.

John: There is this receipt from January 13…

Their eyes locked. Short silence, in the thick of unspoken words.

Jane: I cannot remember what happened on January 13. You will have to give me more than that.

John: On January 13, you went to the bakery. You spent seven dollars and four cents, and you included this receipt as a shared expense. I cannot remember seeing, touching, smelling or tasting that bread. You ate it all by yourself. I am not contributing to the cost.

Jane was speechless. Bread. His grand discovery was a loaf of bread! What could she respond to this? Are divorcing couples now arguing about artisan loaves? Is this a new trend? Jane looked at the expenses file on her phone, and glancing at the list again, she noticed the exact same amount from the same bakery which John had included in the shared expenses file. She couldn't help but smile.

Jane: The bread I bought was for everyone in this house, not just for me. I am sorry you do not remember tasting it. You also have a bill from the same bakery, and it is for the same amount, seven dollars and four cents. This is funny, don't you think?

Their eyes locked again. John and Jane looked angry.

John: Once again, you are mixing up two different situations, and no, this isn't funny. As I've already said, I don't remember the bread you claim to have bought for all of us, because I've never seen it. Unlike you, when I buy bread, I place the loaf on the kitchen counter so it's obvious it is for everyone. What I do remember is that the bread I bought was gone in a day. I gave some to the kids, and I am pretty sure you had some too.

She recalled vividly how the kids devoured the bread she bought at the bakery. She scrolled through her phone to find pictures which would prove she had not devoured it all alone, like some bread bandit. To her dismay, she could not find anything.

Without evidence, that loaf hung over her head, obscuring any chance for an amicable divorce settlement. No pictures. Maybe she could find something else? She concentrated hard, reliving the moment: kids at home, dinner time. No witnesses. The kids were too young to remember what they ate and when.

She lost the bread battle.

Next time, she would be more careful and gather the evidence. Maybe snap pics as the kids ate or feed them in a public place where everyone knew them, like the neighborhood playground. But it was winter, and it was freezing. How could they then eat outdoors for all to bear witness? Plus, would neighbors be ready to testify about kids' diets in court? What was left for her? What practical options did she have?

She conceded to subtract the seven-dollar-and-four-cents bill from the shared household expenses. She hoped this would butter John up a bit. Little did she know, another culinary conflict was waiting just around the corner.

The very next day, Jane accidentally crossed another food boundary that made the bread argument look like a mere appetizer. It was lunchtime and she decided to make herself a salad. She hummed to herself, washing crisp lettuce leaves under the cool tap water. She patted the leaves dry and stepped back. Something was missing. She opened the cabinet, spotting a jar of nuts. Perfect for some added crunch. She sprinkled them liberally over her masterpiece. She did not realize that this jar was John's private stash, the one he gradually built over those past weeks with his personal financial resources. Then, she drizzled her homemade vinaigrette over the salad, giving John's precious nuts an unauthorized oil bath.

John stepped into the kitchen just in time to witness the crime in progress. His eyes widened. His mouth fell open. He stumbled backward, his hand finding the wall for support, as if witnessing a car crash rather than salad preparation. His carefully curated stash was being scattered recklessly over Jane's lunch, and without his permission. John finally managed to gasp, his voice an octave higher than usual:

John: What are you doing?

When Jane realized her error, she stopped immediately and apologized profusely. She then embarked on a painstaking mission to retrieve each nut from the salad and return them to their rightful place: John's nut jar.

Tragically, some of the nuts had already been stained by the vinaigrette, leaving her at a loss for what to do. She stared at the damaged nuts while John was simply frozen, unsure how to react to this act of barbary. He hung there, suspended in uncertainty, as the world around him blurred into the background. His body refused to budge.

In one minute, Jane managed to ruin his precious nuts.

After a moment of reflection, Jane came up with a solution. She counted the damaged nuts aloud and calculated their value at approximately two dollars.

Two dollars for his nuts.

She placed two one-dollar bills on the kitchen counter and left the apartment to go grocery shopping.

Throughout the grocery run, she couldn't stop wondering: Would he take the money? Or would he not?

As she passed the nuts aisle of the supermarket, she felt a twinge of sadness. She shook her head at the realization of what she had become: someone who had lost herself in the relationship, reduced to counting damaged nuts and leaving dollar bills for compensation—as if controlling small things could somehow make up for losing herself.

When she returned home, she had her answer: He took the money. It was not peanuts after all!

John's Journal: "Asked her not to touch my private stash of nuts. Found two dollar bills on the counter and half the jar empty. 150 days . . . Until order is restored."

Jane's Journal: "150 days . . . Until I don't have to provide character references when I eat my lunch."

The musical chairs

Late February. The living room window was open, allowing the fresh evening breeze to flow in. John and Jane were sitting at the dining table discussing an upcoming visit. Her brother Paul was coming to town. John and Jane did not look happy.

Jane: But remember, I told you that my brother would be coming on those dates. I don't understand why you look so surprised.

John: No, you did not tell me.

Jane: Yes, I did. Remember? It was the day when we received the report cards for the kids. After we looked at them, I told you about my brother's planned visit. I told you he would come for one week and that he had found accommodation nearby.

John: This is simply false. This is false. This conversation never happened. That's it. End of discussion.

Jane started reiterating what she had just said. She was immediately cut off.

John: No, no, no, you are lying. If you indeed talked to me, then you must have muttered something, and it was not audible.

Jane: I did say something to you then, but not clearly enough?

John: Stop it, this is enough. You always twist what you are saying to fit your own agenda. It never stops with you. You constantly change. You change your story and the truth all the time. My brain is super simple while you have a super brain, and you are just trying to mess with my head. One thing I know is that you are smarter than I am, and all the time, you are using it against me. You plan for everything; you are always one step ahead. You lied to me by planning your brother's visit without me.

As Jane listened, she thought: *Yes, I do change sometimes, and it is clearly time I change husband.*

A few days after this dramatic episode of sifting through truth and deception, the much-hated brother paid a visit. At that time, in the months leading to the court hearing, John and Jane, our two strangers, were choreographing their weekend parenting duties like a harmonious ballet: entering and exiting the stage gracefully. Jane would take care of the children on Saturday morning, while John would be with them in the afternoon. Sunday would be the other way around. That specific Sunday, John arrived forty-five minutes earlier than usual, to find Jane having lunch in the living room with Paul, Milo, and Mia.

Dear Reader, I must take us back a few years to describe how their dining set-up here came to be, which perfectly mirrored their relationship: mismatched and lacking harmony. Years ago, they purchased a large table with four chairs from a reputable furniture maker. After that, a first high chair was purchased for their firstborn, Milo. Shortly after, Mia popped out and Jane managed to secure two additional high chairs from the neighbor on the floor above them, which this neighbor was kindly giving away. That made for three high chairs for two kids, and Jane initially thought that they would give one of them away to another family in need. But John was impressed by the durability and quality of those wooden kids' chairs, so much so that he claimed one for himself (despite their cramped seating space, as they were not made to accommodate an adult's overwhelming stature). One glorious weekend, armed with a screwdriver, he adjusted the high chair to his own height, ensuring he could dine comfortably at the table. Yes, six-foot-two and in his very own high chair.

Jane could not wrap her head around the fact that her adult husband (they were not yet separated when this event unfolded) would find comfort on a seat designed for toddlers. Would he want a sippy cup too? It was a bizarre blend of funny and frustrating, and she couldn't help but feel that he was again, in his own way, living in a completely different reality—one where high chairs were the pinnacle of comfort.

John's decision to opt for a high chair led to a surplus of two additional chairs in their living room, prompting John's persistent plea for Jane to dispose of two of the four adult chairs to save space. Jane had long resisted, arguing it made no sense to keep a large table with only two adult chairs in their living room. She even suggested that John use an adult chair and donate one of the high chairs. The audacity! Of course, he adamantly refused. Never had he found such a good chair to sit on in his decades of existence. After countless hours of debate over many months, she finally relented; she could not bear to hear about his beloved high chair once again. And so, half of their adult chairs were tossed in the garbage. Their living room was therefore left with two adult chairs and three kids' chairs.

What they did not anticipate was that Mia would insist on sitting on the second adult chair as soon as she turned two years old. She wanted to sit like a "big girl" at the adult table and her wishes were granted. From then on, she proudly took her meals on her adult chair, her chin barely grazing the table, making it a struggle for her to see her plate and eat. A logistical challenge? Sure. But adorable nonetheless.

Back to the story. Like any toddler, Mia was growing up and on this Sunday with her uncle Paul, she finally mastered the art of confidently grasping her fork, guiding it to her plate, and bringing the food to her mouth. All without making a mess. Jane was just finishing preparing lunch for the four of them. It was time to sit around the table and eat, but there was a problem: There were only two adult chairs around the dining table, and both would be occupied, one by Mia and the other one by Jane. Milo was sitting in his own kid's chair, and Uncle Paul was left with two options: John's high chair or Mia's former high chair (which was still adjusted for her toddler height).

The choice was obvious, although consequential. John was still out and would likely be gone for at least another hour. Jane ultimately decided to offer Paul John's chair; it was a kid's chair, but at least the height was adjusted for an adult to be able to sit on it. Deep down, she knew she was doing something wrong. *But what other choice do I have? There are no other options.* One always has a choice and yet again, Jane made a bad decision which would carry heavy consequences. Paul did not understand his sister's internal turmoil and thus sat on John's chair without hesitation. He was amused to be sitting on a high chair for the first time in his adult life.

Drama ensued. Forty-five minutes earlier than expected, John swung the door open with a flourish. The patriarch was home. When he found Paul comfortably seated in his chair, John felt something crack inside. He'd spent an entire weekend adjusting that chair to his exact specifications. The precision brought him joy—finally, something that fit exactly as it should. If only everything in life could be adjusted so perfectly.

He turned livid. A surge of disbelief and indignation flooded his mind. Those two idiots had crossed a line this time—they went too far.

His high chair, his sacred throne, was now occupied by an unexpected challenger. It was evident what this challenger desired: his rightful seat at his own table. Once again, the two siblings were conspiring against him, undermining his very existence and signaling their blatant disregard for his personal space. Enough was enough. He would not be tolerating that type of behavior ever again.

Living room. Uncle Paul calmly eating his meal next to his nephew, unaware of the tragic unfolding of events he would cause.

John walked up to the table and faced Paul.

John: That's my chair, and I will be having my lunch now.

John moved closer to Paul, expecting for him to get up. After a moment of disbelief, Paul stood, eyebrows raised in silent question to his sister. It was a moment to remember. Jane remained silent, keeping her head down. If she looked up now, she would erupt into uncontrollable laughter at the absurdity of it all. Making eye contact with Paul was too risky. She abruptly fled to the kitchen area, and behind the wall, she erupted into silent laughter, pursing her lips and covering her mouth to keep it in.

After a few minutes, she composed herself and graciously walked back to the dining table and its eclectic set of chairs. She was purposely not looking at John, who was chowing down his food on his favorite chair.

Paul was standing next to the dining table, holding his plate and still actively eating while on his feet.

Mia and Milo were looking at the strange scene, amused. Their parents and uncle were making their best efforts to produce a surreal show just for their entertainment.

Jane to Paul: Since you are eating while standing up, I offer you half of my chair. This one is an adult chair, and I am sure it can fit two people. We are brother and sister after all, we need to stick together, both literally and metaphorically.

She thought: *After all, if a high chair for children can fit an adult man, there must be enough space on an adult chair for two adults!*

Paul joined his sister on her large chair, smiling. John rolled his eyes and scoffed, but kept ferociously eating his food, with his anger being channeled at every bite.

And so they ate: five people, five mismatched seats, one last shared meal. Milo in his high chair, Mia proudly perched on her adult chair, John in his modified high chair, and Jane and Paul sharing half an adult chair each.

They were breaking bread together, probably for the last time. Jane studied their faces in the fading light—her innocent children, her fuming soon-to-be ex-husband, her quietly amused brother. She knew with sudden clarity that she was witnessing the end of something. Soon, very soon, this table would divide like everything else in their lives. She savored the moment, bitter as it was, knowing some suppers aren't meant to be repeated.

Soon, she would be leaving this table—and her half-chair—behind.

John's Journal: "130 days . . . Found him sitting in my chair. My chair. The one thing that still felt like mine in this chaos."

Jane's Journal: "130 days . . . Until sitting doesn't require a visa application."

ACT TWO

LET'S GO GROCERY SHOPPING!

Who Ate the Avocados?

John opened the refrigerator door for the third time that evening, hoping the eight avocados might magically reappear. They didn't. He'd specifically bought some for his precious daughter Mia who, at two and a half, still refused to eat anything else. And now, they were mysteriously gone. John paused in the hallway, catching his reflection in the decorative mirror Jane had insisted on hanging there. Was he really about to start another argument over food? Over avocados? He almost laughed at the absurdity of it. But this wasn't petty—this was principle. And principles mattered, especially when everything else in their marriage was crumbling. His jaw tightened, *Jane!*, he called out, already knowing who the culprit was.

John: Funny thing . . . I bought four avocados on Sunday and they seem to have . . . disappeared. I remember that before going to the store, there were four avocados left in the fridge. And now, the fridge is empty.

For the curious reader, who I know pays close attention to details, this conversation took place on a Thursday. That was the fourth night after Sunday, and who knows if John bought the avocados before or after dinner last Sunday. On Sunday, then, there were eight avocados: four plus four. Let's assume all eight were gone. Eight avocados eaten in four days. If evenly consumed, that's two avocados per day (though any smart reader knows daily food intake can vary).

Now that we have gathered all the avocado facts and laid out our avocado assumptions, let's ask the burning question everyone (or at least one half of this unhappy ex-couple) wants answered: How can two avocados disappear from the fridge every day for four days straight? Where did they go? Will we ever see them whole again? Who is responsible, and why?

John was on the case and determined to solve this mystery, at any cost (obviously, without spending more than the cost of eight avocados).

With no solid leads and still no solid food in his stomach, he asked Jane if she had anything to do with it. He watched her reaction closely. Would she twist her fingers like a child who just got caught? Would her lower lip start trembling? Would she look down? Or maybe slightly left? After so many years of life next to each other, he should be able to read her mind. He should be able to know when she was telling the truth and when she was lying. But he no longer knew who she was, what thoughts occupied her mind, or what motives drove her actions. She had become a master at deception. But he would not let himself be made a fool. He knew she was involved in the mysterious avocado disappearance. What other possible explanation was there? It would not be the first time she ate more than she should. Or got rid of the evidence.

Jane's blank face reminded him of another time she'd played innocent. One night, last Winter, he'd caught her swiftly tossing something in the trash. It seemed like a big container, but he could not see what it was at the time. He did not ask, then, as his wife could be very sensitive. He waited until night and when he was sure she was asleep, he sneaked to the kitchen and then opened the trash can. At first, he could not see anything. But he was sure she'd thrown out something unusual!

Undeterred, he rolled up his pajama sleeves and dug into the trash can. He would expose his wife's strange habits. After a bit, he realized the truth was just on top of the garbage bag, but it had appeared so impossible to him that he looked right past the container. Jane had thrown out a whole jar of yogurt! The full jar! A jar which was not even opened! He immediately rectified his wife's terrible mistake and put it back in the fridge, after wiping it with the utmost care it deserved. That night, it was impossible for him to fall asleep. Was it the first time this happened? Or was it just the first time he caught her in the act? How many jars did she throw out over all those years? How many? He lay awake, tossing and turning, contemplating the possibility that his wife might have been repeating this horrific act throughout their almost decade-long marriage, all while keeping him in the dark.

The next morning, he was eager for the alarm to go off. He was itching to confront his wife. After she got out of bed, he asked her about the jar of yogurt. She seemed genuinely surprised by the question. Maybe he'd jumped to conclusions too fast; maybe she had a plausible explanation. Surely, she had one. She would not have dared otherwise. And there it was . . . the explanation! She had the audacity to claim that the yogurt was expired by a mere one day! Twenty-four hours! Everyone knows those expiration dates are flexible. She stuck to her story, making it sound logical that she threw out the yogurt jar, and she acted like he was the unreasonable one for rescuing perfectly good food.

With this tragic event still imprinted in his memory, he knew she would find a conniving excuse for the missing avocados. She was good with her words and out to get him. But this time, he would be strong. He would not be deceived.

So why did he ask a deceitful future ex-wife about the missing avocados instead of solving this mystery quietly? Because he had no leads yet, and she was known to talk too much. She might slip up and reveal the truth inadvertently. John felt like a detective on a mission to crack the case of the missing avocados. As expected, Jane gave an extensive explanation.

Jane: Well, well, Sherlock, let's break it down. I only see two possibilities here. Either I tossed those avocados out on a whim, or they were devoured. Joke aside, let's not treat these avocados like missing people—they are gone, eaten into oblivion. Allow me to walk you through how it went down. Mia and I have been feasting on avocados each day since Sunday, with one avocado each. That adds up to eight avocados for the both of us. I hope this is clear for you now, but please let me know if you need more information.

John paused to process the information. Something was missing from the explanation.

John: Something is off here. There were *eight* avocados in the fridge on Sunday night, and the only day Mia could have possibly eaten them is Tuesday.

When he looked at Jane, he realized she was not following his logic. Or was she deliberately pretending not to understand? He decided to break down the facts he had collected around the avocados' disappearance:

John: You see Jane, Tuesday was the only day when I did not see what Mia had for dinner. And it is impossible that she ate eight avocados in one meal. Therefore, where are the avocados?

He paused for a minute to see how Jane would respond to his irrefutable reasoning.

Jane did not budge. Her face appeared blank, showing no sign of a reaction. How was it possible? Shouldn't she feel some guilt now that she had been exposed by John?

This time, Jane did not feel this familiar tightness in her chest. Jane felt absolutely nothing because there was nothing left to be felt. When she realized she no longer cared about John or his ever-changing stream of accusations, she felt liberated. Then she thought of Mia's favorite character, and she started singing in her head: *It's time to see what I can eat . . . No right, no wrong, no rules for me, I am free! Let it go, let it go, I am the one who ate the avocados!*

Faced with Jane's complete absence of reaction, followed by a mocking smile, John had to do something or say something, anything really, to grant him the honor of concluding this suspenseful detective case.

John: Well, I'll let it slide this time.

John smiled. The dramatic tone he used was glorious. John's conclusion brought singing Jane back to reality. Wait, no argument this time? Had he given in despite his knowledge of her insatiable appetite? Was it finally acceptable for her to eat more than one avocado a day? Jane admitted to herself she had pushed it too far. Eating that many avocados during a contentious divorce process while still living with her ex under the same roof—what on earth was she thinking?

He'll let it slide this time, Jane thought, fighting to keep her expression neutral. *How generous of him to pardon a peasant like me for stealing from the royal garden!*

She pondered if things would have been different had she just given him a heads-up about her dinner's plans. After all, communication was key, especially since they would co-parent soon. She probably should have strived for transparency, open communication, and trust. Instead, she sneaked behind his back, even taking one avocado for her lunch at the office! What if her colleagues were called to testify about her avocado theft in court? She hoped that the coworkers she had lunched with on this fateful day would soon be transferred to an international office.

In the next few months, John and Jane would go to court. Could our two strangers move past the avocado treason? Could trust ever be restored? How could John be sure that Jane would not eat more than she should again?

John married a petite woman for a reason, and now this?

Jane was breaking his trust; she was breaking their food contract.

That night, Jane could not sleep. Was it guilt or the excessive avocados churning in her stomach? Down the hall, Mia slept soundly. In her dreams, avocados grew wild and plentiful. No one counted them. No one claimed them. They simply existed to be enjoyed. Her small fingers twitched in her sleep, reaching for green treasures that belonged to everyone and no one.

John's Journal: "120 days . . . I try to keep track of what the kids eat—is that so controlling? She ate their avocados and won't even admit it despite overwhelming evidence."

Jane's Journal: "120 days . . . Ate an avocado. Apparently committed a felony."

Tomato Tom-ah-to

Bad stuff always seems to involve tomatoes. It either starts with a tomato or ends with one.

Remember what happened to that comedian who bombed on stage? Tomatoes. And that politician who couldn't keep a promise? More tomatoes. Have you heard of the imperfect wife who boycotted the tomatoes section in the supermarket throughout the entire winter season? You guessed it—Jane. Not one single tomato in her grocery bag for four months straight! The question on everyone's mind (well, John's mind): Was this a culinary protest? A nutritional stance? Or just another creative way to drive him crazy?

John: Look, I know this isn't the first time I've asked, but it's becoming urgent now. Can you please grab some tomatoes? It's your turn for grocery shopping this week, and the fridge is looking like a desert.

Jane sighed. This was the third time this week that John had brought up the tomatoes. Jane was starting to regret suggesting they alternate grocery shopping responsibilities every other week now that they were separated. Before she asked for a divorce, she had handled the shopping almost entirely on her own, and John never commented on the contents of her grocery basket. Jane mistakenly took his lack of complaints as an endorsement of her shopping skills.

On his first solo shopping expedition after they agreed to the alternating grocery schedule, John discovered a world Jane had apparently been hiding from him all these years. He was welcomed to the store by enchanting music and the most ravishing smell. Probably a mix of on-site bakery fumes (doughnuts? muffins? colorful birthday cakes?) and floor detergent. He took a deep breath, as if he could already tell this evening would represent a milestone in his new life. He picked a cart carefully (not all wheeled carts are created the same; some show enhanced maneuverability relative to others). From this moment on, our modern Aladdin started freewheeling through endless aisles, all displaying diamonds in the rough. For the first hour, he was unable to pick anything for his cart. He was simply exploring this whole new world, roaming through the aisles, absorbing all the magical wonders and treasures on the shelves. Treasures he had never seen in the fridge of his home. Treasures which were probably on display in the aisles only today. Just for him. How lucky was he to go shopping at this unique moment in time! He returned home triumphant, his bags brimming with items that had never before crossed the doorstep of his house.

Two weeks later, it was John's turn to go grocery shopping again. John returned to the same supermarket on a magic cart ride, only to find—surprise! —the same treasures still staring back at him from the shelves. He did not immediately grasp the serious implications of his discovery. Slowly, as he was venturing through this whole new world, realizing it was not so new after all, the reality began to dawn on him: The wonders he discovered two weeks ago were offered every single day, and Jane never picked any of those delightful items to bring home. Ever. How dare she?

The ugly truth was that Jane was a terrible shopper.

How had he not seen her complete lack of shopping skills before? Was she genuinely terrible at shopping or was she just cruel for withholding such culinary beauty from him and her own offspring? He caressed the pitted prunes, the dried apricots, the coconut-covered dates, the cranberries, the almond-cashew mix, all stored together in this one single location, this dazzling place he never knew existed. How many new meal horizons would have been possible if only she had brought a piece of this new world home? Did her dullness prevented her from having a truly explorative magic cart ride? Or was she just being mean and selfish?

The tears welled in his eyes as he stood in the fluorescent-lit aisle, haunted by the memories of years filled with tasteless meals. He thought about all the times he had choked down uninspired dinners, believing that this was the norm, never realizing the culinary marvels that had been within his reach all along. The weight of his own ignorance pressed down on him, and he wondered how he could have been so blind. It wasn't just about the food. It was about all the moments he had missed, the opportunities for joy and discovery that had slipped through his fingers. His eyes were now wide open, he had come so far and would not go back. As he wiped his tears away, John made a silent vow: Never again would he leave such an important part of his life to chance. He would take control, not just of his grocery shopping and the contents of his fridge, but of his destiny.

Taking back control from his inconsiderate wife would start at this very moment. John wanted tomatoes and he wanted them now. He had shown kindness and patience as he had already asked her several times. This was her week to go grocery shopping. She obviously did not buy enough food, and her basket did not include tomatoes. She had to buy those. Not just for him, but for Milo and Mia as well. Poor kids! What would they be eating this week? John was standing in front of Jane, maintaining eye contact and waiting for her to respond. He would not let it go this time.

Jane: I already went to the store last Friday and spent eighty-five dollars and thirty-four cents. I kept the receipt, you can check. I've already explained to you that the supermarket downstairs does not have good quality tomatoes in the winter. But I did buy plenty of fruits and veggies, eggs, bread, yogurts, turkey and a few other things.

There was no immediate response from John, leaving Jane to wonder whether she should have been more specific in her grocery list rundown. Eggs were straightforward, always a dozen. But had she chosen free-range or organic? Such an obvious question he could be asking! And yet, she didn't have the answer. What would she respond if he asked? She was literally walking on eggshells here. It was a fifty-fifty chance. Would she risk being wrong? Pick one at random and risk being called a liar again? Or admit she didn't check the quality of what she routinely bought? What a terrible mother she must be!

And how many slices of bread were in a bag? How many mornings before the slices were all gone, averaging about five slices a day? And those red apples, were they Honeycrisp or Gala? Maybe Pink Lady? So many questions without answers. She should have been prepared. But she wasn't. Now she would have to face the consequences. Her mind wandered back to a morning in the early 2000s when, after breaking her usual habit of studying every day, she was caught off guard by a surprise biology test. What did she do then? History was repeating itself and unfortunately, she never learned from her mistakes.

She took a deep breath and awaited John's response. Maybe he would not ask any questions.

While Jane was lost in her thoughts, John was absorbing all her revelations in silence. There was something soothing about watching her defend her grocery choices. For a moment, it felt like before—him teaching her the right way to do things, her listening. He missed those intimate moments. When suddenly, the silence was broken and the verbal clash resumed. As always, John and Jane did not look happy.

John: There will not be enough food for the week. Can you please go back to the store?

Jane was at a loss for words. She should have been more specific about quantities and provided a thorough list. Milk! She forgot that. Pasta too.

But wait, this conversation was just surreal. It did not make any sense. They were two adults after all, right? Jane smiled (her dazzling smile, of course). She was unsure if she should retreat from the conversation, try to defuse it, or lean into it.

Jane: Oh, is it because you're craving tomatoes? Poor thing! What will you do without your tomatoes?

Here she was, joking again! He was bringing up an important health issue and she was taking it lightly, as she always did. John was furious.

John: The tomatoes are not for me; they are for the kids. They always eat tomatoes. Why did you stop buying tomatoes?

Jane was taken aback. John was not joking. This allegation was serious; he was suggesting that there has been an abrupt change, and that the children's routine lacked consistency due to the absence of tomatoes in the fridge. She had to provide a swift response to defend her integrity.

Jane: Actually, the kids don't eat many tomatoes in the winter. I have all my receipts from this season if you want to check.

Then, she grinned mischievously.

Jane: Feel free to "peel" through my receipts. You will see there has been no abrupt shift in my shopping habits—it's just seasonal adjustments.

John was not responding. Jane could feel he was scrambling to think up another rebuttal to continue this conversation. A conversation which had already lasted way too long. The truth was, Jane had learned about seasonal shopping from her father, who taught her that the best tomatoes come from summer gardens, warmed by the sun. Some lessons stick with you, even when everything else is changing. She wished she could explain this to John, share this piece of her history, but they'd lost the ability to really listen to each other somewhere along the way.

More importantly, they couldn't even discuss anything that mattered: their separation, their future, their children. But here they were, peeling through her grocery receipts and debating whether failing to buy tomatoes in the winter should be considered a serious offense. This was such a waste of time and energy. All she wanted was to be alone on her medium-firm mattress in the living room. This conversation had to stop at once.

Jane: To be completely transparent, I know for a fact that spring is coming near. I will therefore be making some changes to my shopping basket in the coming weeks to include more seasonal produce, including bright and delicious tomatoes. How does that sound?

John didn't respond, his jaw tightening almost imperceptibly. Jane stood to leave, then paused at the doorway.

Jane: You know, you can fight with me about groceries all you want, but you can't argue with the seasons. Some things just take their own time—tomatoes, divorce papers... everything ripens eventually.

Jane had won the tomatoes round.

As the silence stretched between them, both knew what remained unspoken. These weren't battles about tomatoes or grocery lists—these were quiet struggles for solid ground as everything else shifted beneath their feet. With each day bringing them closer to the courtroom, they clung more desperately to the small decisions they could still control.

But next time, Jane vowed to be more prepared, with all her grocery knowledge and details at hand. She would be ready for the interrogation when the topic comes back on the kitchen table.

John's Journal: "No tomatoes in fridge. Again. She has started a tomato resistance movement. Refuses to buy them in winter. 110 days . . . Until winter tomatoes reclaim their rights."

Jane's Journal: "110 days . . . Until I never have to justify my produce choices to the tomato police."

Team bread versus team cereal

Jane loved these April mornings. Sunlight spilled into the kitchen as she spread jam on toast. This almost felt meditative, and for a few minutes, she could forget about divorce papers, court hearings, and the six-foot-two man across from her sitting on his high chair. Milo and Mia ate their yogurt quietly, faces still puffy with sleep. Her coffee was steaming just in front of her; and she would be taking her first sip once the children's toasts are ready. This breakfast routine was probably the last normal thing in their life.

John seemed preoccupied. Perhaps it was the fact they were going to court in less than three months? Or was it something far more serious? Jane quickly dismissed this thought. John's concerns were no longer hers. She started spreading jam for her own toast as she heard John's voice.

John: Can you please go back to the store and get cereal for the kids? We are out and it is your turn this week.

Jane: I already did the grocery shopping last weekend and picked up a ton of bread—enough to last the whole week for breakfast. If you want cereal for yourself, feel free to grab it.

John believed in cereal. It was what kids should eat for breakfast. Changing breakfast routines felt like changing the laws of physics. Jane was raised on toast. Simple bread, warm and familiar. Their breakfast battle wasn't just about food—it was about two people who had never lived in the same world, even when sharing the same kitchen.

The new John would not give in and be defeated so easily. The next day, John asked again about the status of the cereal acquisition.

John: Have you bought the cereal?

Jane: No.

John: Can you get cereal? And also yogurts for the kids? We have run out, and it is your turn for grocery shopping this week.

Jane sighed heavily as she considered this befuddling request. This did not make any sense. Her kids were not eating cereal every day, and she was sure she bought several different yogurts when she went shopping last weekend (she actually bought fifteen!). She gracefully glided to the fridge and swung it open. The light from the fridge cast a divine glow around her strikingly beautiful face.

Jane: I don't understand your question. I did the grocery run last weekend and spent one-hundred-twenty-four dollars and thirty-six cents. Check the receipt yourself. Among other things, I got fifteen yogurts and three loaves of bread. And look up here on the top shelf . . .

She started counting, reaching eight. Eight kids' yogurts were left while he just said they had run out! What a find! She belly-laughed. She knew there were a few yogurts left, but eight! That was more than enough for the rest of their week. She had not felt that happy and satisfied for a very long time. Eight yogurts—she could get a trophy for Super Mom, couldn't she? She had bought enough vitamin D for her kids to support pursue their growth for one full week. Hooray!

Faced with this flawless argument, John shifted his focus to what he deemed was his primary concern, which was and always had been the cereal. Why did he bring the yogurts into the conversation without checking the facts first? This amateur mistake took them off track; she used this to her advantage and won the yogurt battle. He had to regroup fast and launch the next offensive. One of his greatest strengths was his persistence and she would get tired of it at some point.

John: Great about the yogurts. But what about the cereal? I have been asking you for days and you are just messing with me. The kids have cereal every morning. We have run out. Last weekend was your turn to shop. So, I am asking one more time: Can you go to the store and grab some?

Jane took a deep breath.

Jane: You asked for yogurts and cereal. I am telling you, we are not low on yogurts. And as for cereal, the kids do not eat it every morning. Usually, it is either bread or cereal, and most times it is bread, especially if they are having breakfast with me.

John did not respond. Jane thought this absence of a response was odd. Was the cereal debacle really over? What else did he have in store for her?

The next morning, Jane found a pink Post-it note on the fridge. It read: "I bought a pizza for the kids which I am planning to give them this weekend. It is in the freezer. It is not for you to eat." Apparently, her recent cereal crime had inspired him to expand his food responsibilities all the way to the frozen section.

On her way to the office, Jane could not help but think about the sweet words her ex wrote for her.

"It is not for you to eat."

She almost missed her subway stop at the evocative thought of devouring the forbidden pizza.

"It is not for you to eat."

She arrived in the office lobby and stepped into the elevator. The doors closed and she was alone in the elevator cabin. She sighed wearily, the phantom scent of pizza teasing her senses, as if it were wafting through the air.

"It is not for you to eat."

She swiped her employee card to enter her company's floor, walked to her desk, and started working on her computer. Occasionally, the background image on her computer would randomly change. But on this day, she experienced the most incredible coincidence. The background image was a landscape photograph from Naples, Italy, the land of pizzas. This was a sign: Should she defy the Post-it note and feast on the out-of-reach pizza later tonight?

"It is not for you to eat."

She had a lot of tasks to accomplish at work but staying focused that day was a struggle. Her colleagues assumed it was because of her long and complicated divorce process. Little did they know the reason was a simple frozen pizza. Simple but forbidden. Would she? Wouldn't she? Would Jane, the Eve of modern times, dare to sneak a bite at the forbidden frozen pizza, strictly off-limits, when she got home? Would she be able to resist the seductive aroma of the "fresh" frozen food? She had always had a soft spot for melted cheese encased in ice. Honestly, frozen food in general had always been a weakness of hers. When she went grocery shopping, she often found herself lingering in the frozen aisle, savoring the refreshing chill that made her feel like she was skiing in the Alps.

With frozen food, time stops, and can re-start anywhere, anytime. Some chefs somewhere prepared this exquisite pre-made meal, and she had full control on where and when to eat it. But since she was a "good" mom, she also bought lots of vegetables, and her go-to was the mixed vegetables bag. This choice was itself a mixed bag—Milo liked peas, not carrots, Mia liked carrots, not peas. And their preferences often swapped, like a shared custody schedule of who likes what.

Fast-forward: Jane never touched the pizza. But she did move it slightly each day—just enough to make him wonder. Psychological warfare, frozen food edition. The "cold war" had officially begun.

Two weeks later, the cereal issue resurfaced during breakfast. When John brought it up, Jane was caught by surprise. She wrongly assumed it had been put on the shelf of all the topics never to be discussed again. Once again, she underestimated John's persistence. However,

Jane did not want to play that day. She stood up, left the table, went to the supermarket close to their building, and bought herself out of the cereal game. Ten minutes later, Jane was back, a box of Cheerios in hand.

She placed the family size Cheerios box on the table, in front of John, and looked right at him.

Jane: So, that settles it. No need to bring it up again.

John: I brought it up because you systematically ignored me. All I did was remind you to go back to the store for the cereal you forgot to buy in the first place.

He paused.

John: I also remember you saying that you did not like cereal and that you did not eat cereal.

Jane frowned. Where was this conversation heading? And would it last longer than the tomatoes debate? Will they be discussing cereal until their court hearing? And should she bring a Ziploc bag of Cheerios to the judge as evidence of their post-relationship failure? If so, should she bring the plain ones or the colorful ones? John's voice snapped her out of these thoughts.

John: So, you say you do not like cereal. And then what do I see? You eating them directly from the box I bought for the kids last week?

Jane closed her eyes. She thought she could buy herself out of the cereal fiasco by buying that five-dollar-and-ten-cent box of cereal. She had hoped to bury this shady affair swiftly and quietly. But oh no, he wasn't falling for it. He was far too sharp. He saw right through her and her schemes. He knew she had eaten cereal for breakfast while she'd claimed to only eat bread for breakfast in America—land of the Pop-Tart, home of the waffle. Who was she kidding? This country worshipped breakfast diversity: pancakes drowning in syrup, eggs fifteen ways, peanut butter sandwiches, crunchy cereal oat, donuts, cupcakes . . . Her bread-only stance was ridiculous, and they both knew it.

She felt so stupid.

She could not fool him. But how did he know she ate from the box he bought? When was it again? Seven or eight days ago? Who spilled her secret? She never entrusted even closest friends with this dark and nutty aspect of her life, as she wanted to shield them from the weight of such knowledge. Then, if nobody knew, how did he become aware that she would occasionally snack on the Cheerios left on the countertop? She would need to be more cautious in the future.

He must have caught her around six a.m., just before everyone's alarms went off. She had been enjoying the serenity of the living room, where she had set up her cozy medium-firm mattress on the floor, wrongly assuming the space was hers before everyone emerged from their bedrooms. That day, she slipped out from under her cozy duvet, threw on a sweater, and briskly walked to the kitchen. That was her private time, ten blissful minutes spent alone with the sunrise. The first light of day bathed the countertop, drawing attention to a large, golden box. She thought, why not? I have ten minutes; no one will ever know.

She grabbed a bowl and poured the tiny rounds Cheerios, cascading from the box like a fountain of eternal youth and new beginnings. The clicking of the Cheerios made a delicious sound, as they each struck against the porcelain of the bowl (or was it tarnished purple plastic?). For this brief breakfast rendezvous, the fridge hummed along in harmony, adding to the melody as she crunched on the forbidden food.

It was glorious.

Then suddenly, a loud noise. Jane jumped. Who was it? Relief washed over her as she realized it was just the hiss of the heating kicking on. She was so scared of being caught that she burst out laughing. And then, she kept on eating.

That was probably when he saw her.

John's Journal: "90 days . . . Discovered disturbing evidence of direct-from-box cereal consumption at 6:07 AM. No bowl. Cereal levels declining. She denies all cereal infractions. What's next—drinking milk from the carton?"

Jane's Journal: "90 days . . . Of providing alibis for missing cereal flakes. Soon, I can eat breakfast without providing sworn testimony."

Sisyphus, or the myth of grocery shopping

Editor's note: Sisyphus was a devious king condemned by the gods for eternity. His crime? Hubris and deceitfulness. His punishment? He was forced to repeatedly roll a boulder up a hill, only for it to roll back down every time he neared the top—symbolizing a never-ending cycle of futile effort.

One Friday morning, in mid April, Jane shopped at the store conveniently located next to their building complex. Perhaps she could have waited to get groceries until Saturday, but she boldly defied the unwritten grocery timing rules by stocking up right before the weekend started. Fast forward to the following Thursday at 10:55 a.m., precisely six days post-shopping spree, Jane received a meticulously crafted email from John.

John's email read: Hey, just a reminder, it's your turn to handle the grocery shopping this week, like we talked about yesterday [Wednesday] and the day before. We ran out of yogurt for the kids yesterday, and Milo wasn't thrilled when I told him so. The only fruit we have left is bananas, and we are completely out of tomatoes and cucumbers. Can you swing by the store soon? We are not going to make it through the week like this!

It was not just any email: It was a masterful composition outlining John's grave concerns about the family's risk of starvation over the next two days. This seemed a tad dramatic, even for John. Clearly, something else was boiling underneath—likely a grudge about the tomatoes incident. Perhaps, if she had just bought those tomatoes when he asked, this madness could have been avoided. Perhaps, they might have even settled their differences outside of court? Oh, the underestimated power of fresh veggies and their potential to alter life's course! Court was less than three months away.

After a couple of readings, Jane began to doubt herself. Was John right? Was last week's shopping so insufficient that she was about to invite Famine into their home? Thankfully, she was working from home that day, so she mustered her courage, marched to the fridge, and swung open the door to assess the situation. To her relief, the fridge wasn't empty. She was not putting anyone's life in danger. Jane wondered how she'd ended up in a marriage where even buying bread required a PowerPoint presentation and every small decision required full justification.

She went back to her desk, sat comfortably on her chair, and began crafting a response to John's email. She felt like the eighteenth-century Marquise de Merteuil responding to the daily letters of her amoral lover-turned-rival Vicomte de Valmont in *Dangerous Liaisons*, a French novel set in the private, decadent salons of the French aristocracy in the years leading up to the Revolution. Jane started writing:

Dear Lord John,

As I wrestle with the demands of my busy day, I find myself compelled to respond to your burning questions, though I must apologize for the delay. As a Lady of the town, I am burdened with numerous obligations, and an entire village relies on me. Yet, fear not, my lord, for I remain devoted to you; every fleeting moment of free time I possess is devoted to addressing your inquiries.

I must confess, I am rather surprised by your newfound interest in my grocery basket since I declared our entanglement must come to an end. Is it that you perceive this as our final season of sharing the contents of our fridge? That these are the last moments to gaze upon my purchases, my meals, and my wanderings? If this is indeed the case, I must implore you to abandon such indulgent thoughts. Forgive my boldness, but you must forget me. We must place the tomatoes where they rightly belong—in the beautiful garden of our memories. We have traversed this relationship for as long as we could, but there is simply nothing left around the avocado pit.

In a recent conversation with the gardener, I learned that the Dollar Store shall host a grand ball this Saturday, by invitation only, to celebrate its opening. My curiosity piqued, so I ventured to the venue to take a glimpse at it, and I was fortunate enough to meet the gentleman in charge. He graciously extended an invitation, along with a five-dollar coupon, valid for seven days with a minimum purchase of fifty dollars.

My lord, I present to you both the invitation and the coupon; I trust you will attend and, perhaps, as you seek an object to purchase with the coupon, you may uncover your new muse among the attendees.

You have posed a question, and I shall answer you with the full truth that you deserve. How I wish I had confided in you sooner.

Yes, I confess, I shopped on a Friday. In my defense, I had not anticipated that such a lapse in judgment would yield such dire consequences for our family's survival. I usually shop on Saturday, but this particular Saturday, a conflicting obligation—or shall I say, a pleasure—beckoned me to the massage salon. You must believe me, my once beloved, that this indulgence had not occurred since the birth of our second child. My weary bones cried out for relief, and I succumbed! I slipped away in secrecy. Oh, forgive me for my sins!

Thus, I found myself at the market a day early. I spent a total of seventy-four dollars and thirty-five cents. Though the details may be somewhat blurred by the subsequent massage, I believe my Friday haul included milk, yogurt for the children, bread, cereal boxes, fruits, and vegetables. And yes, your cherished tomatoes as well. I have preserved the receipt, should you wish to verify my claims.

Tomorrow is Friday, the day before it is your turn to venture to the market. Pardon my reasoning, if it seems flawed, but it strikes me as natural that the fridge would not be fully stocked six days after my market visit. It is not full, but it is far from empty. I would never permit our fridge to resemble a barren wasteland. Before I wrote to you, I gazed into our fridge, which remains vibrant: a splash of yellow from bananas, the greens of lettuce, a hint of orange from baby carrots, and the rich reds of apples. The scene struck me as peaceful and beautiful, and inspired me to create a drawing in the style of my favorite artist Van Gogh. I have enclosed it here. I hope it brings you joy.

Yours truly,

Lady Jane.

Jane chuckled at the thought of writing such a letter. Naturally, she wouldn't do that. Instead, she composed a brief email that captured the essential points. But she included a charming picture of the fridge as evidence. It was not a van Gogh, but a well-lit, high-quality photograph from a flattering angle.

Never did she imagine she would one day be documenting her refrigerator's contents. Little did she know, this seemingly mundane act would become a cornerstone in the next installment of our story.

John read the email a couple of times. He noticed the picture of the fridge as evidence of its contents. He smiled. He had taken a picture of the fridge the night before. Though he didn't want to reveal his hand, he felt it was time to share it with Jane. Unsurprisingly, his picture looked much better. He drafted a brief email response and attached his photograph.

John's follow-up email reply read: Last Friday the fridge was full, but you still went shopping. Spending ninety-four dollars on groceries doesn't go far for a family, especially when you're buying from the pricey market next door instead of somewhere like Aldi or Costco. By yesterday, we were already out of a lot of things. Honestly, it's no surprise the fridge ended up like this—just take a look at the picture below. Does that seem like enough to feed two adults and two kids?

There was a lot to digest in John's latest email.

But first, Jane examined the picture he had attached. It was of the fridge again, but from a different angle. A fridge always has two sides, and it is important to consider both before forming an opinion. Before delving into the details of the email, Jane compared the two images of the fridge: hers and his.

In her photo, Jane had arranged the food like a magazine photo shoot: labels facing forward, bananas, apples, and lettuce positioned to look plentiful in flattering light. She'd carefully framed the shot to show only the well-stocked areas.

John's photo captured the same fridge as a barren wasteland, with empty spaces highlighted, produce spread as much as possible, and a lonely Tupperware marked "JOHN'S LUNCH" sitting in sad isolation next to three baby carrots.

Going from one picture to the other felt like flipping through a children's picture book, transporting her back to her own childhood. Her thoughts drifted to her mother, a strong, resourceful woman who tirelessly shopped for her family in a time long before grocery delivery services existed. She recalled her mother's smile, adorned with a few missing teeth because she prioritized her children's needs over her own. Despite her natural elegance and beauty, she never pampered herself with luxuries like dental crowns, preferring to sew her own clothes and style her hair with expired butter. Her mother saved on everything, finding creative solutions where others saw only limitations. Even her wedding dress found new life as winter scarves and diaper cloth. She crafted her own jewelry from oyster shells. She charged her cell phone at the post office to save money. She was truly extraordinary. As Jane reflected, she realized she could never measure up to her mother's selflessness and ingenuity.

Her thoughts wandered back to the present, when the absurdity of John's email sharply contrasted with her memories of a simpler time.

She read through his initial and follow-up emails again.

1. Jane faulted by choosing Friday for grocery shopping, instead of Saturday or Sunday, messing up with the unwritten rules for grocery schedule.

2. Jane faulted by not buying enough food.

3. Jane failed to shop at grocery stores that he approved of.

As she reviewed the two emails for probably the tenth time, Jane wondered if there was a secret list of approved supermarkets they were supposed to adhere to. With all the texts they were routinely exchanging, she could have easily missed one. Should she feel guilty for her lavish lifestyle, born out of convenience? After all, her routine trips to the local grocery store conveniently located next to her apartment complex had been a reckless drain on the family's finances. The average urban family spends one thousand and eighty dollars per month on groceries, totaling approximately sixty-five thousand dollars over five years. If the stores John mentioned were indeed twenty percent cheaper, her careless expenditure would add up to a staggering thirteen thousand dollars!

Couldn't she simply walk for thirty minutes and carry the bags like any responsible mother would? Did her relentless pursuit of efficiency really justify this lack of financial prudence? She had no valid excuses. But would she improve next time? (Spoiler alert: She would not.)

A few weeks later, in early May, John sent yet another email, nearly identical to the previous two, as the situation seemed to be repeating itself. Hadn't Jane learned anything at all?

In this mere remix of what she had just endured, this time with a grocery bill climbing to one hundred-and twenty-four-dollars, John, true to form, unveiled a snapshot of the fridge as damning evidence that her efforts had once again fallen short. It felt like a game of pickleball gone awry, with each player relentlessly smashing the ball at the other, fueled by discontent at having to play together.

Fast-forward to the end of the one hundred and twenty-four dollar pickleball match. Evening had fallen, and our two strangers were standing in the living room, which Jane had annexed a few months earlier. They did not look happy.

John: For four people, and you brother's appetite, it just didn't cut it. Let's avoid ending up in such a situation in the future.

Guilty as charged! Jane's brother Paul was in town to visit her and the kids (again! Because apparently that's what brothers do—support their sisters during difficult times and sit on their ex-husbands' chairs), and he was staying at an apartment nearby. Jane had the audacity to invite him over four separate days when she knew John would not be home. John never saw Paul on those occasions, but he suspected he had come—less food in the fridge told its own story. With Jane's numerous sneaky invitations, John found himself unwittingly subsidizing half the cost of the five meals she had with her brother in his home. Yet, just as Jane was beginning to lose hope, she remembered one crucial detail that could save her case.

Jane: Since you've raised the issue of my brother Paul, let's break this down a bit to soothe your concerns. This week, we ate out for lunch every day, which means I didn't pack my usual homemade meals like we both typically do. So, by that logic, whatever food from home

I didn't consume at lunch, my brother feasted on for dinner. Ta-da!

John was boiling with indignation. Her words left him momentarily speechless: He would not be able to debunk her implacable reasoning. But she was wrong! Deeply, morally wrong . . .

Given John's lack of an immediate response, Jane tried again, reformulating her long-winded justification. But John knew better. How dare she? Feeding her brother, the very same brother she knew John could not stand, in his home, at his expense, and probably again on his own high chair? The audacity! This wasn't a careless offense. It was calculated, that's for sure. She wanted to destabilize him, weaken him for the next battle.

What was she strategizing next? He was afraid to find out. But soon, fear gave way to fury. How many clandestine dinners had taken place under his unsuspecting nose? Two? Three? Perhaps more than three? Reining in his temper, John strived to have the last word.

John: If your idea of shopping includes six pots of jam in your one-hundred-and-seventy-four-dollar grocery bill, then sure, you technically went shopping. But that's not real food and this is certainly not enough to feed the kids for the week.

Here we go again. *Shall I go back to the store to put an end to this conversation?* Jane thought. *But then, what would happen the next time I shop? It would all repeat, wouldn't it?* That's when the realization hit her—she was a modern Sisyphus, damned for eternity or at least for the remainder of this union. Instead of rolling a stone up a mountain, she was hauling endless grocery bags filled with tomatoes, yogurts, and cereal boxes. No matter how much she brought home, it would never be enough. She would constantly have to return for more. Some fruits might spoil, requiring yet another trip. The ones that stayed good would be devoured too quickly, necessitating yet another haul. And all the while, she would think about the cycle repeating endlessly. She wondered: *When am I finally getting out? When is my court hearing?* Unlike Sisyphus, Jane's punishment had an expiration date.

John's Journal: "85 days . . . She continues shopping at the overpriced store next door. No bulk discounts. No rewards points. She even paid FULL PRICE *for organic eggplants. Financial emergency declared."*

Jane's Journal: "85 days . . . Until I don't have to share my grocery shopping list for peer review."

Finally, a little bit of art

What do you do when you want to prove to someone you are right? What do you do when words are not enough?

You take pictures.

You capture life in precise moments and share them – your truth, raw and unfiltered. For John and Jane, their truth was Art. Unknowingly, our two strangers were building a masterpiece together. For months, they exchanged photos of the most unexpected muse: their fridge.

Yes, their fridge. Most people share pictures of their kids or their pets—not the contents of their refrigerator.

This had never been done before. A fridge, a mundane yet vital part of daily life, was transformed into something poetic and grand. Think about it: What's the most essential appliance in the kitchen? It's the fridge. It preserves your fresh food, nurturing health and growth for everyone in the home. And hidden within it is the freezer, always ready to help when meal preparation time is scarce.

The fridge rarely gets the credit it deserves. We vehemently curse at it when it breaks down, yet do we ever celebrate its unwavering service when all runs smoothly? Do we realize how lucky we are to have it by our side, every day of our lives? John and Jane were no different. They were either slamming its door (especially Jane, who was a little wild) or ignoring it entirely. But one day, as their marriage unraveled and divorce loomed, they found solace in their overlooked companion, their fridge. And as they opened the door of the refrigerator, light poured forth—so much light, so unexpectedly beautiful.

While most people capture sunrises, sunsets, or the aurora borealis, John and Jane photographed something far simpler yet equally profound: the light inside their fridge. Together, they discovered a shared passion for this unexpected style of photography.

As their court date approached, the photographic exchanges intensified. John discovered that standing on a chair provided the perfect overhead angle to document nutritional neglect. His brother received an unexpected midnight text: *Do you think this looks empty enough? Be honest.*

Jane found that her phone's portrait mode could blur the backgrounds of her fruit displays. Her brother received an unexpected midnight text: *Should I arrange the yogurts in color order or by expiration date?*

Sadly, their collaboration ended when Jane moved out, leaving behind an album of extraordinary photos of their fridge's contents, a time-lapse of their marriage dissolving one grocery item at a time.

If future anthropologists dug up this odd collection of fridge photos, what would they learn about divorce in our time? They might discover that even when breaking up, people can't help but create something together. In the emptying shelves of their fridge, they'd find the story of two people who captured their breakup more carefully than their wedding day, transforming grocery battles into accidental art, and turning what they lost into something neither expected to create.

John and Jane's Journal: "84 days . . . We've documented the fridge contents with more care than our wedding photographer showed capturing our first dance. Future civilizations will know exactly how many yogurt containers remained on our final day together."

ACT THREE

RUN, RUN, RUN!

Epilogue: The rise of the dolphin

Fast forward to beginning of August, after the much-awaited court hearing.

It had been two weeks since Jane moved out. Two weeks since the judge had ruled. Two weeks of sleeping in a real bedroom with four sturdy walls and an actual door. Two weeks of feasting on avocados if she wanted to. Two weeks in a place that felt like home again. Her happiness radiated there, and her children glowed in response. She could see it in their eyes: They were relieved to see their mother happy, just as she was relieved to see them happy too.

So, how did John and Jane start their new lives happily never after? Well, they each went on great vacations. Per their custody agreement, John would spend a week off with the children at his family's house (Jane would take her week with them later in the month). As the weekend approached and Jane realized she would have seven days completely to herself—something she hadn't experienced in over a decade—a wild idea took hold of her.

What would I do if I could do anything? she whispered to her reflection as she brushed her teeth. The woman staring back at her looked different somehow: lighter, with a spark in her eyes that had been missing for years.

Jane had never travelled alone. Ever. Family vacations with her parents, spring break trips with friends, and then, of course, vacations with John and the kids.

Get properly settled in her new apartment? Nah! Go somewhere? Yeah! Where? Anywhere by the beach where the water is warm. The thought wasn't something she carefully considered; it just came to her naturally, rising up from a part of herself that had been sleeping for a long time. And just like that, Jane decided to embark on a solo vacation. She was ready to begin her new life under the sun and palm trees.

Just two weeks after the court hearing and signing of their separation agreement, Jane was on a plane, wedged into a cozy middle seat as she'd booked her flight last minute. During the flight, Jane couldn't help checking her phone repeatedly, scrolling through photos of Milo and Mia. Milo with spaghetti sauce all over his face. Mia wearing Jane's too-big sunglasses. Milo's attentive face when he was diligently cutting hundreds of sheets of paper. Mia's serious face when she "read" books upside down. Her heart squeezed with each swipe.

She'd never been away from them for a full week before.

She closed her eyes and leaned back in her seat. A familiar tightness gripped her chest, but beneath it, a certainty: This was right. This was necessary. She could almost hear their voices in her head, their high, sweet voices chanting love songs they'd invented just for her. That was the most beautiful music she'd ever heard.

Finally, the plane dropped through clouds. Jane caught her first glimpse of turquoise water and her throat tightened. Other passengers looked out with casual interest. Just another trip for them. But for Jane, that blue stretch wasn't just a vacation spot. It was the edge of her new life. The beginning of everything.

As she stepped off the airplane and felt the warm breeze on her face, tears streamed down her cheeks. But this time, they were not tears of pain or anger, they were tears of joy. She had done it. She was out, and she was finally about to start a new chapter of her life. A chapter in which she would be the author, not just the actress. A simple chapter, uncomplicated and easy to write, in which her characters would simply be, happy.

At the airport, she waited for her suitcase to arrive on the conveyor belt. Nearby, a couple bickered quietly about whether they should have taken an Uber instead of renting a car. Jane smiled to herself. Memories of her past life.

When her new, bright pink suitcase finally rolled into view, she exhaled in relief. Finally! That was it. Her luggage was not lost, and her new life was about to start in the most uneventful way. She gripped the luggage handle and felt grateful. Grateful to be among those women who have a job, a bank account in their name, and the financial stability to make their own choices. Grateful to have built a safety net for herself, because freedom often comes with a price.

With her suitcase firmly in hand, she stepped out of the airport and into the sun.

Remember the book *Eat, Pray, Love*? Well, she did something similar—minus the praying. But that's a story for another book.

The resort where she stayed was a lively hub of colorful characters, a real kaleidoscope of life unfolding before her, as diverse as the sea life she had the pleasure of discovering on a snorkeling tour. With a friend she met at the resort, someone with laughing eyes and an easy smile, Jane found herself people-watching from beach chairs, cocktails in hand.

Jane, hiding her smile behind her glass: See that man by the pool bar? Total pufferfish. Harmless until someone takes his lounge chair. Then—boom—he puffs up like he's about to explode!

Friend, laughing: And that woman teaching everyone salsa? Pure angelfish. Graceful, shimmering, drawing everyone into her orbit.

Jane, watching the sleek man glide from one female guest to another: Look at the resort manager over there! Total swordfish. With the bride-to-be, he is all romance expert. With the businesswoman on her annual retreat, suddenly he's discussing investments. Maybe tonight, he will tell me he was the one who invented the mojito?

They continued, playfully matching guests to sea creatures: the honeymoon couple never more than an inch apart like twin clownfish, the old professor by the bar with stories as twisty as an octopus, the little kid who splashed everyone like an enthusiastic baby whale.

Later, as they walked along the shore at sunset, the waves gentle against their ankles, Jane turned to her friend with curious eyes.

Jane: My turn now. What fish am I?

Friend: No doubt, you are a dolphin.

At first, Jane was disappointed. Dolphin seemed like such an obvious choice. A bland answer. Was she that plain?

Friend: Ah hah, after going snorkeling with you and seeing your swimming skills, I can safely say you are a land animal! You barely managed to keep your face in the water! I said dolphin because dolphins symbolize freedom. They are playful and social, but they also chart their own course. They surface for air when they need it, dive deep when they want to. Everyone lights up when they spot one. Have you ever seen someone sad to see a dolphin?

Jane did not quite catch the full explanation. All she heard was "freedom." That was the first word her friend said.

Freedom.

That word resonated deeply with her.

Later that evening, she stood alone on the beach, watching stars appear one by one. Like a dolphin breaking the surface after a deep dive, she was ready for her next breath.

Get ready, girl!

Mid-May. Jane, the soon-to-be dolphin, was soaking in the bathtub of the family apartment she still shared with her ex. To relax, she counted the bubbles floating calmly in the water—bubbles that, much like her life, seemed to pop the moment they reached the surface. In her bath, Jane also counted the number of days until the court hearing that would hopefully allow her to move out. 51 days. It seemed surreal that maybe, just maybe, in less than two months, she'd be soaking in a different tub. A newer tub. A happy tub. But what if no court ruling was made? What if their case was dismissed to a later date? A bubble popped.

As soon as the judge issues the order on the custody schedule, I am out of here, Jane vowed, glaring at a lone bubble as it burst. John would never leave this apartment; she knew that much. If she wanted her freedom, she had to be the one to go. Legal proceedings rarely follow a straight path. While the judge would establish child custody at this first hearing, the matter of who would keep the family home could drag on for years, potentially. And if John had proven anything over the years, it was that he was as immovable as a boulder in a stream—he will never willingly leave. Jane, meanwhile, was more than ready to leap like a dolphin, breaking through the surface and soaring toward a new horizon. If she wanted her freedom right after the first court hearing, she would have to be the one to go. But where?

For weeks, every night after putting the kids to bed, Jane would scroll through real estate listings to find "the one." She would swipe through countless listings, each one promising a perfect match at first glance. But alas, just as quickly as she found a potential gem, disappointment would strike on the first date. On many occasions, the pictures posted online did not match the actual apartment. The real estate broker would say they were referring to another apartment they had in their portfolio which had "similar qualities." Exhausted with her search and frustrated with all the fake advertisements, Jane reached a breaking point and told her broker: *Imagine this is online dating. Imagine I portray myself as five years younger and I post pictures of my gorgeous sister. We meet. You are obviously disappointed, and I tell you that my sister and I share similar qualities and similar parents? How would you react?* In addition to the fake advertisements, Jane had to deal with the dreaded apartment ghosting: those places which seemed too good to be true and vanished from the market without a trace. After a while, Jane started to learn how to crack the code: Apartment listings boasting "stunning natural light" probably meant a single, awkwardly placed window, "cozy bedroom" was often code for tiny space where one could make the bed, close the door, and open the window, all without taking a single step. And what about those "amenities?" Was the alleged gym the staircase which would need to be used every time the clunky elevator from the fifties required maintenance?

Jane kept swiping right. She never lost hope in her quest for "the one." And one day, just like that, she found it. Pouring sunlight, plenty of space for her and her kids, and a brand-new building elevator. It was love at first sight. The apartment even had had a move-in date aligned with her court date. It was meant to be. She signed the contract that same day. Stars were aligning and the once-cloudy sky was clearing up.

Now that she had secured a place, it was time to prepare as much as possible for the move; but she had to do it without raising suspicion. John did not know she had found a place. He would probably be furious that she found something *behind his back*. She also did not want to already concede that she would be ready to leave him the apartment. For some reason, she wanted to keep him in the dark about who would need to move out of the shared apartment and who would get to stay.

To move out, one needs moving boxes. Jane thoroughly researched the market of moving boxes. Apparently, moving boxes these days can set you back a whopping one thousand dollars, especially if you order them last minute. Fortunately, she lived in a large apartment building with a spacious refuse room for trash and recycling in the basement. It was a goldmine of discarded cardboard boxes.

Each day, with the zeal of a treasure hunter and the discerning eye of an art connoisseur, Jane embarked on her cardboard crusade. At first, she grabbed every box in sight, scooping them up like a kid on a sugar high in a candy shop. But over time, she grew picky, oh-so-picky. Jane was no longer content with just any old box. She craved perfection. It wasn't enough for a box to merely exist; it had to speak to her. It had to captivate her senses, not just with its look but also its smell, while enticing her with promises of sturdiness and structural integrity.

Jane became a box detective, tapping, analyzing and scrutinizing like Sherlock Holmes solving the Case of the Cardboard Crown. And oh, when she found *the one*! There was a sparkle in her eye, as if she had stumbled upon a diamond in the rough of bubble wrap. This box, the masterpiece, would be the next turret of her cardboard castle. And Jane, in all her cardboard-collecting glory, smiled with satisfaction: *Today was a good day*.

Slowly but surely, Jane's cardboard castle took shape, box by box, next to her medium-firm mattress, which occupied *two-thirds of the living-room space*. Each box she rescued from the basement wasn't just cardboard; it was a piece of her future.

John watched this empire grow, eyes widened in disbelief and perhaps with a tinge of envy. For there stood Jane, guardian of boxes, resilient and mysterious, ready to make a move. *But which move? What's her plan? What is she plotting with all these boxes? Is she starting an Amazon delivery service out of our living-room to pay a part of her divorce legal fees? Or is she just testing how much clutter I can tolerate?*

One day, unable to bear the suspense any longer, John finally asked Jane about her fortress and pointed the box which was the closest to him.

John: What is this?

Jane: That? It's a standard 16 by 12 by 18 inch box with double-wall construction and a 30-pound weight capacity. It was delivered to Mrs. Smith on the tenth floor last Tuesday.

She paused and added casually:

Jane: Maybe it contained a small robot vacuum. Or vintage records. Or a drone. Or a karaoke system. Or a cotton candy machine.

John: But what are you doing with all of these boxes from our neighbors?

Jane, ever cryptic, replied with maddening simplicity.

Jane: When we go to court, the judge will decide who stays and who goes. The boxes are here and ready to ease the moving process when it comes. I don't know who will be filling those boxes—you or me. But someone will have to leave, and now, they'll be able to leave fast.

John blinked, momentarily convinced it might be him. But how? Could Jane force him out legally? Was there something she knew that he didn't? Impossible! His lawyer was more expensive than hers: Surely, he was the one with the upper hand. That question alone still cost him two hundred and fifty dollars in legal fees. After the conversation with his attorney, John was left more confused than ever. Jane's plans were shrouded in mystery, and whatever she was cooking, it wouldn't be bland.

By June 1, Jane declared her crusade complete. No more daily trips to the basement; her cardboard kingdom was built. Court loomed near and Jane was ready.

But a fortress of boxes was only half the battle. Leaving also meant packing those boxes. Her most precious belongings needed to be packed and safely stored away from the apartment before the court date—just in case. Of course, she couldn't take too much out of the apartment; that would raise suspicion about her concession to leave the place to him. What to take and what to leave behind? She needed to set priorities and map out a clear plan before putting it into action. With only a couple of hours to get it done, there would be no time for hesitation.

To complete the delicate mission, Jane waited for John to leave for the office. Once she was certain she had the apartment for herself, she sprang into action—armed with a giggle and a roll of moving tape, she tossed dresses and jackets like confetti into boxes labelled with friends' names. She then hopped from cab to cab, scattering her belongings in the city like breadcrumbs. Friends' closets became safe havens for her treasures, far from John's potential clutches.

I will guard your shoe collection, but my roommate will likely stage an intervention about shoe addiction.

I will guard your trendy dresses, though my mother will keep asking when I have developed actual taste.

I am keeping your diamond safe, but my boyfriend is asking which engagement I'm planning to accept first.

Jane had good friends. After successfully smuggling out her third box of belongings, Jane realized she'd created noticeable gaps in the closet. Standing in front of the half-empty space, she pictured John's suspicious face examining the barren hangers. No, this wouldn't do at all. Even John would notice something was up. She needed a solution. Kneeling beside her bed, Jane pulled out storage boxes untouched since their second move together: baggy sweaters, worn cardigans, and shapeless tops she had kept "just in case". Today was that case.

One by one, she hung those fashion time capsules in place of her favorite clothes, creating the illusion of a full closet. John, a spiritual man who was oblivious to material possessions, never noticed how colorful dresses and fancy jackets were swapped for old sweaters in his apartment's closets.

Jane was done for the day. She fell onto her medium-firm mattress, a quiet sense of accomplishment settling in. She knew her precious boxes would soon be reunited with her, in her new place, to begin a fresh chapter with style and grace.

John's Journal: "30 days . . . Can't find the couch under the cardboard mountain. She adds more boxes daily. I am trapped. She's enjoying this."

Jane's Journal: "30 days . . . Until my cardboard castle becomes a real home."

Divorce day, part one

This is it. On the morning of the court hearing, our two strangers' alarms rang in perfect sync at 6:15 a.m. Jane smiled from her living room mattress. How fitting that on this final morning, even their wake-up calls seemed to acknowledge the occasion. Like starting pistols at a race, their identical alarms launched them toward separate finish lines.

After the usual morning chaos, Jane finally got the kids onto the school bus. The apartment fell blissfully quiet. John had disappeared right after the kids, no doubt heading to his favorite café for his double-shot Americano. She had the place to herself before their 9:30 appointment with destiny.

Jane, the soon-to-be ex-wife to be, couldn't help but smile. Today was the big day. What does one eat on divorce day? She opened the fridge, surveying her options with newfound lightness. *Eggs?* she wondered aloud. *Too heavy for court.* Her eyes drifted to the cereal box. She smiled, remembering the long-standing drama.

No need to indulge in those forbidden flakes today. *Alright, bread then? Yes, bread it is. Bread is always a good choice.* She needed just enough to fuel her through the morning, but not so much that her carefully chosen dress would feel tight and uncomfortable. She patted her stomach, satisfied but not stuffed, ready to step into her outfit and into her new life.

Jane caught her reflection in the hallway mirror: tired eyes betraying nights spent staring at the living room ceiling and wondering what would happen. No time for that today. She needed to look put-together.

In the bathroom, she reached for her foundation with a slightly trembling hand. It went on flawlessly, and she made sure to avoid creating a line around her neck that screamed, *I'm wearing foundation three shades too dark.* Then came the concealer, applied like a criminal hiding evidence of her past mistakes.

Next came the eyeliner. A tricky beast, but she focused on the task. She would draw the perfect wings, ready to fly her into her new life. Today, she would also have the fake eyelashes she loved so much to get this extra wow factor. After all, you don't go to court asking for divorce every day.

A quick sweep of blush warmed her cheeks with a glow that months of tension had stolen. And the lipstick? A bold red, her color. Jane caught herself wondering if she might catch someone's eye at the courthouse, then laughed softly at the absurdity. After all, courts were practically crawling with single men, all eager to fill the position which just opened in their home.

Hair time. She curled it into soft, romantic waves, each strand falling just right. A few strategically placed pins held everything together, with a touch of hairspray to keep it all locked in place. As she looked in the mirror, she saw a former bride ready to dazzle—beautiful, confident, and maybe just a tad too glamorous for a court room.

She hopped on the train to the courthouse. When she got there, the building was not open yet, and there was a line. Jane noticed John, already waiting in line. He was wearing his tuxedo but had swapped the bow tie for a regular tie. He looked excited. After all, this was his day too.

At nine, the courthouse doors opened. They proceeded to the waiting room on the second floor. It was grand and imposing, with high ceilings and marble floors that echoed every footstep. The air was thick with history, each piece of decor telling a story of justice served through the ages. The benches, made of dark, shiny wood, were as unforgiving as the reality Jane had left behind. No cushions here, just hard surfaces to remind you of your humble place in life. Each bench was bolted to the floor; there was no escape.

Suddenly, the double doors leading to the judge's chamber swung open. This was their moment. Our two strangers made their entrance with the utmost grace.

John entered first, with his attorney by his side.

Jane smiled to herself. *How many times in your life do you get divorced?* This was a unique moment, a moment to remember. Especially since they did not think of hiring a professional photographer to immortalize the occasion. She regretted that a bit. After all, she was all dolled up, in a beautiful room with lots of natural light.

Fortunately, Jane quickly dismissed those thoughts. *No regrets. Enjoy the moment. Take it all in.* And just like that, Jane entered the courtroom in slow motion, with her attorney by her side. In her mind, she was trailed by white doves, and flower children with chocolate-smeared faces, tossing legal papers instead of rose petals.

She paused dramatically, took in the audience (mostly clerks and maintenance techs fixing the air conditioning leak), and then sat in silence, satisfied.

John watched Jane's entrance from the corner of his eye. Her confidence rattled him. He couldn't look at her directly, like staring at an eclipse. He fixed his gaze on a water stain on the ceiling. Safer there. He straightened his already-straight tie. Was this room always this warm? What was his role here anyway? The attorneys would handle everything, though he wasn't entirely clear on what that entailed. The maintenance crew were working on the air conditioning unit. When would they fix that ceiling leak?

The attorneys began their opening arguments. The judge listened, asked questions and then took the two attorneys into an adjacent room for further discussion.

John and Jane were left alone in the magnificent court room, under the watchful eyes of the clerks. They avoided eye contact like two strangers on a first date who knew they had no future together. Or did they?

After twenty minutes, the judge and the attorneys returned. Our two strangers had not moved an inch. The judge laid out recommendations for child custody and financial arrangements that both parties accepted. Since Jane had already found her own apartment and just agreed in court to let John keep the family home, the major decisions were set. Now they had two weeks to resolve all remaining minor issues and return to court with a signed agreement.

John's Journal: "She took a SELFIE on the courthouse steps. A SELFIE."

Jane's Journal: "First profile pic of my new life. No high chairs in the background."

The couch, or just half of it

With custody finally established by the court, Jane was technically free to escape to her new apartment. The judge knew she'd found a place and agreed to let John keep the family home. But there was a catch: Their separation agreement remained unsigned, with just two weeks to finalize it before they appeared again in front of the judge.

Jane faced a dilemma: move now and risk triggering a battle over kitchen mugs and throw pillows, or wait until all paperwork was signed? She knew John would want to discuss absolutely everything at excruciating length. One argument about who got the coffee maker could derail everything that actually mattered.

Her new apartment was ready, its empty closets practically waving her over. But was immediate freedom worth the potential chaos? For now, she would stay put and delay the move.

Unfortunately, nothing went according to plan. Days passed with no word from John's attorney. They hadn't even begun negotiating the agreement. Jane's anxiety grew with every unanswered email. Their court date was just five days away.

She had to do something—anything—to feel progress. And what better way to break the stalemate than a trivial squabble over the small stuff?

Jane, a spreadsheet enthusiast, created an Excel document of their household assets. It wasn't something that necessarily required their attorneys' involvement. She cataloged everything from kids' beds to curtains, even items of dubious sentimental or financial value (the bath toys made the list). She proposed what seemed fair, suggested John could offer his own split, and added they could settle disputes with a coin toss.

In the children's bedroom, she offered John the kids' beds, mattresses, dresser, armchairs, and curtains, while she would take the playmat and the kids' play-table. But John dismissed her proposal with the effortlessness of swatting a fly. Jane tried with another room. Same response. She realized they would never agree on what she could take.

The real issue wasn't curtains or playmats, it was time. Their final court date loomed just five days away, and negotiations hadn't even started. Jane understood she'd wasted enough time waiting. Whether she stayed or left the apartment wouldn't change anything now. John simply didn't want her to take anything.

She had to move, and it had to be now. For nights, Jane had rehearsed the move in her head, mentally cataloging what she'd take and leave behind. She calculated packing times and studied John's work schedule: She'd have a solid eight-hour window.

On Thursday night, Jane lay awake on her medium-firm mattress, staring at the ceiling of the living room she'd claimed months ago. Her cousin, Peter, was in town. Trustworthy, strong, and available tomorrow. She typed a message, deleted it. Typed again, deleted again. Was she really going to do this? The thought sent adrenaline rushing through her body.

Every morning on this mattress felt like hitting reset on the same exhausting day. The mattress seemed to whisper she'd never leave, that she'd be negotiating over avocados and cereal boxes forever.

Jane took a deep breath and sent the text.

Jane: I am doing it. I need you tomorrow morning. We are moving out.

Peter responded with his trademark efficiency: Be there by 8 a.m. After sending the text, she fell into a deep, dreamless sleep.

Jane woke up at dawn with a jolt of electricity coursing through her veins. Today was her moving day.

With no moving truck and only two sets of hands, the plan was clear: pack light and move fast. Stick to the necessities in this fast and quiet disengagement. She transformed from Diplomatic Jane to General Jane, mentally mapping out the day's mission with military precision.

But beneath the strategic commander lurked Jane the dreamer. As she surveyed the apartment, her eyes lingered on the pull-out couch. *Pack light, sure—I have no choice. But what if we could at least take that couch?* This magnificent beast, a gift from her parents, was something she was really hoping to bring to her new home. When Jane shared her hopes and dreams with her cousin, he wasn't thrilled. Peter, ever the pragmatist with his engineer's mind, immediately started calculating angles and doorway clearances.

Peter: Jane, you realize we'd need to disassemble this entirely. That's at least an hour of work, maybe more.

But Jane's determination won him over. Peter sighed but smiled. That's how it always went with them. Sometimes Jane proposed the crazy plans, sometimes Peter did; but they always followed each other into trouble. Thirty years of this dance, and neither had ever let the other down. When one called, the other showed up—no questions asked.

It would be tricky, given the limited time, but with two pairs of hands and some strategic thinking, it was doable. They would need to dismantle the couch and probably take two cabs to move all the pieces to the new place. Reassembling it could wait until later in the week when they had more time. Without wasting a moment, they got to work, armed with Jane's new pink screwdrivers (she had proudly bought her first toolbox—a bright pink one—just last week). The couch was made of several parts: the cushions, the mattress, and the frame.

Cushions and mattress? Easy. The two cousins loaded them in a cab and dropped them off at the new place. But then came the frame.

This part of the disassembly was challenging but their determination was unwavering. Peter approached it like a puzzle, methodically working from one end to the other while Jane bounced between different sections, attacking whatever screw looked most vulnerable. They steadily unscrewed the screws one by one, inching closer to victory over the furniture . . . until the couch frame had other plans. One stubborn screw refused to budge, defying every twist and whispered plea. They tried absolutely everything.

With time ticking away, they faced a dilemma. Do they admit defeat and leave the couch frame intact, while the mattress and cushions were already at Jane's new place? Or should they dedicate more time and try again?

Peter: I think this is time to move on . . .

Jane: One more try!

Jane squeezed behind the couch, one foot against the wall, the other on the frame. Pink screwdriver gripped like a dagger. Jane twisted with all her might, one last time. The screw stayed put.

Practicality eventually won over pride.

Jane: I guess the couch won this round . . .

The two cousins abandoned the dismantling effort and decided to leave the skeletal frame in the middle of the old apartment, a monument to their failed mission.

Instead of frustration for not being able to move the full couch (with the frame), laughter filled the room. Jane and Peter chuckled at the absurdity: cushions and mattress triumphantly relocated to her new place, while the frame stood its ground, a lonely sentinel in the wreckage of her old life.

John, amused: Half a couch is better than no couch. Besides, you got all the soft parts!

Jane stared at the skeleton of the couch in the living room. Just the bare frame, stripped of comfort and warmth, yet stubbornly standing there. It reminded her of what her relationship with John would become—

stripped down to basics but impossible to completely take apart. The couch frame would stay with him; their children would keep them connected. Just at a more comfortable distance.

Shaking off those thoughts, she turned to a more practical question: Would John insist she take the remaining frame, or could it become an unintentional parting gift?

Only time, and the whims of divorce court, would tell.

The toilet paper heist

The living-room now featured a lonely couch frame and dozens of moving boxes. The couch debacle had already eaten up two precious hours, and the clock was ticking. They had to hurry to move the rest of Jane's belongings.

In a whirlwind of chaos and giggles, Jane and her cousin Peter executed the fastest move-out in history. With no plan (other than "let's figure it out as we go") and no moving trucks in sight, they embarked on a taxi-fueled adventure. Whatever they lacked in preparation, they made up for with determination. They frantically filled the building's moving cart with whatever they could carry, pushing it to the street and debating the most optimal time to call a cab. Should they book it inside the elevator? Right before taking the elevator? Or after getting out? And how big of a car did they need? Could their haul possibly require an XL? Everyone knows an XL cab takes longer to arrive, and every second mattered.

Every trip in the cab felt like a rollercoaster ride of nerves and laughter, racing against the clock. They needed to be done before John got home from work. Jane couldn't take the frame of the couch, obviously. What about the coffee table and the rug underneath? Those were easy to pack. And the three mirrors? Absolutely. Keeping those trophies was victory enough. Everything else could stay behind.

Six cab rides later, the two cousins took one last look around the apartment. All of Jane's personal effects, the coffee table, the rug and the three mirrors had been moved to the new place. Their job was finally done.

What about all the things from her old life she wouldn't be taking with her? Tables, chairs, lamps, dressers— she bid them a quick farewell, as though they were old, expired store coupons. Jane was embracing her minimalist future with full peace of mind.

They evaluated that they probably had thirty minutes or so left. They could squeeze in one more trip, Jane thought. The last one. It had to matter. She looked at Peter. Their eyes locked. In this unique moment (all moments are unique by essence, but this one was "really unique"), Jane and her Peter shared a silent and telepathic moment. With eyebrows raised and a nod that could launch ships, they wordlessly agreed: One last trip, and they would hit the jackpot of essentials. Game?

The list was strategic: half of the Swiss chocolate bars, half the pasta, half the rice, half the laundry detergent (exactly half, because despite her spite she harbored for her ex, Jane wanted to do it by the books).

Jane was lost in thought, her mind wandering through the chaos of the move, when suddenly she remembered—of course, the toilet paper rolls! It was an essential she couldn't leave behind! But those rolls were much too long to count and split evenly! It was therefore an all-or-nothing choice. She carefully considered the two options. Being a woman meant she needed those essentials more than John did.

She fondly recalled an old parenting debate from about a year ago, on a Sunday morning, and the infamous "one sheet of toilet paper lecture." John had noticed Mia using "excessive" toilet paper and realized that they had missed the lesson on proper paper usage when they potty-trained her.

John: One sheet, Mia, always one sheet. It is all anyone needs, properly folded.

Jane had nearly choked on her morning coffee.

Jane, to John: Have you ever actually used just one sheet?

John had puffed up like a proud peacock.

John: I've been a one-sheet man my entire adult life.

The debate escalated until Jane challenged him to a demonstration using a glass of water and his cherished one-sheet method. The resulting mess had required half a roll to clean up. John had looked genuinely offended, as if she'd questioned his life's research. Jane countered with evidence from women worldwide and was about to launch an anonymous Facebook survey to women around the world before they both eventually let the matter drop.

Ah, those intellectual debates—she would miss them dearly! He was a true *household expert* with an opinion on everything and always shared his deep thoughts with his beloved wife. Remember the time he brilliantly suggested toasting bread in the oven (rather than buying a new toaster) because it used gas they didn't pay for, rather than electricity which was their charge? Such wit, such deep thoughts!

And yet, for all his expertise on household economics and bathroom efficiency, John had never once in seven years together purchased a single roll of toilet paper. He'd stroll into the bathroom, blissfully unaware of its origin, as if the toilet paper fairy visited while he slept. Did he think rolls magically reproduced themselves in the dark linen closet? He probably didn't even know how to change an empty roll, always leaving that bare cardboard tube behind for the little fairy to deal with.

No, this wasn't stealing. This was toilet paper justice.

Peter snapped Jane back to reality. They had a time crunch, no time for daydreaming.

Peter: So, what do we do?

After a dramatic pause, General Jane made her most audacious move yet.

Jane: Help me load the cart. We're taking them all.

Peter froze, leaning back in disbelief.

Peter: All the toilet paper?? Isn't that a bit…

Jane, with a grin: What? Petty? Childish? Brilliant?

Peter: I was going to say "bulky", but sure, let's go with brilliant! So, one last time: are you sure?

Jane laughed, a full belly laugh.

Jane: All. Well, except one pack. For the kids. Let's not go *that* far.

Jane, opening the linen closet: We need a system for stacking them all in the cart.

Peter, reflecting: Let's start with the three jumbo packs. They go on the bottom for structural integrity. We'll pyramid it with a wide base.

Jane: Right. Pass me the ultra-soft single rolls, these can go in the edges. We can also crisscross each layer to stabilize.

They stacked with the same intensity they'd had as kids building Jenga towers, hyper-focused, tongues slightly sticking out. Each roll placed with surgical precision.

Jane: I have more, we need to go higher.

Peter: Careful, it's getting wobbly on level five.

Jane: Just a few more, here . . .

Jane stuffed three more rolls into a tiny gap. Once all rolls and packs, except one, were loaded, they stepped back to admire their masterpiece. The toilet paper tower now rose nearly three feet above the cart.

Two adults stood before their toilet paper pyramid. Peter snapped his measuring tape while Jane took a picture to immortalize their extraordinary accomplishment. A moment of reverent silence fell as they let the glory sink in. It was absurd. It was magnificent. It was unnecessary high. It was unnecessary altogether.

They pushed the cart together out of the apartment and toward the elevator. Just as they rounded the corner, Mrs. Brown from apartment 5B appeared, waiting for the elevator. Her eyes widened at the cart overflowing with toilet paper.

Jane, solemnly: Just preparing for the next pandemic.

The elevator arrived with a cheerful ding. The three squeezed in, Jane and Peter stabilizing their precarious tower of rolls.

Lovely weather we're having, Peter remarked to Mrs. Brown, who stared straight ahead, pointedly ignoring the toilet paper mountain.

The silence was deafening. Jane bit her lip. Peter studied the ceiling. When the doors opened at the lobby, Mrs. Brown practically sprinted out. As the doors closed, Jane and Peter erupted into uncontrollable laughter.

Jane: Did you see her face?

Peter, wiping tears of laughter from his eyes: Next pandemic? Jane, we're five years past 2020. You are about half a decade late to that excuse!

They finally reached the parking lot, victorious with their pyramidal white treasure. As they stood waiting for the cab, the cart now overflowing with toilet paper rolls ready for transport, Jane couldn't shake the nagging feeling that she'd forgotten something important.

But what? She could not put her finger on it. As they stood in the parking lot, waiting for their final cab to take this bounty of bathroom supplies home, it hit her. *The olive oil! The extra-virgin olive oil!*

One last heist. It would be the final piece of the puzzle. She sprinted back to the apartment, taking the elevator with the urgency of a secret agent on a high-stakes heist—every move calculated, every step decisive. Her mission was clear: Snatch the bottle and make it out undetected. This was her final, most daring move. The fate of future meals depended on this. She was running and dodging imaginary obstacles of her own making; they still had a bit of time and after all, this was still her apartment. Jane arrived at the door with the utmost urgency and snatched the bottle of liquid gold from the kitchen counter.

That was it. She felt whole. The essentials were secured. Like Queen Elsa in *Frozen*, she turned away and slammed the front door of the apartment.

Peter was already waiting for Jane in the cab. Jane jumped in confidently, the victory bottle in hand. She could already picture her first dinner party in the new apartment—friends lounging on her couch cushions on the floor, passing plates of pasta glistening with this very olive oil. *To the Grand Escape,* they'd toast, while she'd dramatically recount her move. The toilet paper pyramid would stand proudly in her living room, her only art installation for now, and she'd make a game of having guests guess exactly how many rolls she'd liberated from the bathroom of her previous apartment. The winner would receive a single roll, ceremoniously presented with a bow.

Peter's Journal: "Just another Friday helping my cousin dismantle furniture and fill her fridge while her ex is at work. Perfectly normal family support."

Jane's Journal: "Day 1 in new place. I have cushions, but no frame. John has the frame but no cushions. Divorce in a nutshell."

When John realized his toilet paper was gone

When John came back from work and realized that the mirror of the entrance hallway was missing, he was absolutely horrified. What had she done this time? As he walked into the apartment, the skeleton of the couch greeted him like some haunting relic of their relationship. Reality hit him like a ton of bricks—Jane had moved out. And of course, she'd taken some of the apartment's things with her.

How could she? They hadn't agreed on anything—at least, not as far as he was aware. He had refused to engage with her sneaky Excel spreadsheet that meticulously divided up their possessions. But now, he wondered: How much had she taken? Where was the coffee table and what happened to the cozy rug underneath it? What else had she stolen? He pictured her plotting the heist, meticulously choosing which items would inflict the most emotional damage.

That night, he stayed silent, unwilling to reach out. He wasn't about to give her the satisfaction of knowing just how upset, shocked, and rattled he was by this latest act of aggression. They were supposedly negotiating an amicable separation ahead of the next court hearing, and there she was, stealing the couch cushions!

The next day, John finally broke. He sent her a text asking for the mattress and cushions back, or for her to remove the couch frame at her own expense. Jane wasn't about to cave. She figured it would be too expensive to pay someone to cart away the frame of the couch, and she had almost left everything behind. To him. As for the cushions, she decided she would use them as a makeshift couch in her new place. That's what she told him. What she didn't say, however, was that she found it hilariously absurd to keep half a couch.

Yes, you read that right: In the throes of a bitter divorce, Jane had decided to claim half a couch. How did she stoop so low, you wonder? And how on earth did she manage to find triumph in such a petty act?

A full week had passed when John, mid-business on his throne in the bathroom, reached blindly for the toilet paper. His fingers grasped at empty air. He sighed. He had to sit up and look under the sink. Nothing. He had to head out of the bathroom and open the linen closet. Nothing. Nothing? It wasn't just one roll that was missing.

ALL THE TOILET PAPER WAS GONE!

His initial confusion turned into a tsunami of rage. How could she? How devious! He paced back and forth in his now toilet paper-less bathroom, him, the self-appointed guardian of all things which had ever belonged to this apartment. His thoughts started to spiral. *She did this on purpose. She knew exactly what she was doing. She planned this and set me up to be caught off guard when I needed it most! It started with the couch cushions, the coffee table, the rug, and the three mirrors. Now this! What's next?*

It was the story of his life—people taking what was rightfully his, leaving him to pick up the pieces. His mother had always said people would take advantage of his generosity . . . Now even toilet paper wasn't beneath Jane's scheming . . . John felt his breathing quicken. He must start a methodical inspection of every bathroom supply. He checked the shampoo and body soap, toothpaste, Q-tips, and anything that could have been taken. Relief; all levels seemed adequate. He sighed. Everything was still in its proper place, still under his watchful care.

Like this, he could pretend nothing was really changing. But that night, he couldn't sleep. He could feel Jane's presence, as if she were still there, plotting her next move. He could almost hear her triumphant chuckles echoing through the walls of his now toilet paper-less domain. Meanwhile, Jane was living it up in her new apartment, surrounded by toilet paper rolls and toasting to her freedom with extra-virgin olive oil.

The next morning, still toilet-paper-less, John snapped. This nonsense had to stop.

He had to recoup his rightful property.

He texted Jane: *Can you return the toilet paper rolls you "borrowed?"*

Of course, Jane did not respond to John's desperate attempt to get toilet paper justice. Jane's toilet paper heist had already become a legend among her friends, a reminder that in the post-breakup world, sometimes it's the little things that make the biggest impact.

John's Journal: Declaring state of emergency brief. She's taken the toilet paper too. Not just the olive oil. This meticulous attack on household supplies suggests months of tactical planning. Should have seen the signs when she started buying groceries on Fridays instead of Sundays. Ten days before the final court hearing and the end of this nonsense.

Jane's Journal: Some women get the house in the divorce—I got the toilet paper. Ten days before the court makes it official.

Divorce day, part two

Two weeks after the first court hearing, John and Jane would find themselves back in the courtroom, each waking up in their own apartment this time around.

The night before the final hearing, Jane barely slept. Despite the upcoming court date, their separation agreement was still nowhere near complete. Days had passed with minimal communication between the attorneys, just short emails and unreturned phone calls. Would they have to reschedule? Would the judge lose patience? What if John suddenly objected to what was agreed at the first court hearing? Her anxiety spiraled with each unanswered question. The only clear instruction her attorney had given her was to make a list of everything she wanted to take from the apartment, since she was entitled to half. This list would be included as an annex to the separation agreement which was still under negotiation. Jane knew she wouldn't be able to add anything else—John, true to self, would simply refuse. So, she listed only what she had already moved out during the one-day expedition with her cousin: her personal effects, the coffee table, the rug underneath, the three mirrors, and . . . the couch cushions and couch mattress. She laughed out loud when she typed this: "couch cushions and couch mattress," not "couch." She could almost picture a lawyer in a serious voice reading it aloud: *And to Jane, we hereby grant . . . half a couch.* For sure, it would be caught. Surely, that would be caught. Surely, this ridiculous furniture clause wouldn't make it into a binding legal document.

Morning came. Jane stared at her puffy eyes in the mirror. No amount of concealer could hide a sleepless night. She put on her signature red lipstick. She opted for her navy pantsuit and comfortable flats. No heels today. Court days drag on forever. Her new kitchen welcomed her with silence. Just peace. She sipped slowly, before waking up the kids for school. More than anything, Jane wanted today to be final. Done. Over. The endless back-and-forth had drained her completely. Sign the papers. Walk away. She was ready for this chapter to close. Actually, beyond ready. Exhausted.

The subway ride felt almost mechanical now. Second time this month making this journey. Off at Central Station, up the courthouse steps, through security with practiced ease. She knew exactly where to go. Second floor. Right at the water fountain. Second hallway. Room 201.

When they arrived separately in the judge's chambers, the judge promptly dismissed them to the hallway, since their agreement had not been finalized yet. The judge instructed them to work it out with their attorneys promptly and come back later. Both attorneys cleared their agendas: An agreement would be reached by the end of the day. The attorneys would shuttle between conference rooms all day. Jane in Room A. John in Room B. Going back with offers, concessions and redlines.

Picture the scene: a backdrop of serious legal deliberations, two poised lawyers passionately debating the finer points of their separation, John trying to look sharp with his tuxedo and matching tie, and Jane. Jane doing her best to look as serious as the situation demanded. But all she could think about was the couch.

The meticulously drafted clause specifying she would retain the cushions and mattress, but not the frame. The frame? Well, that, legally speaking, would be someone else's problem.

As the proceedings unfolded, with weighty discussions on alternating vacation calendars, split of the childcare costs and financial disclosures, her mind kept drifting back to the couch. Would they catch it? Would they notice the sneaky maneuver buried deep in what seemed like a simple list of furniture? In her mind, it wasn't just about the couch anymore. It had become a symbol of autonomy, a small victory in the midst of the complexities of divorce proceedings. Who knew that such a seemingly trivial clause could carry so much weight?

On her way to the water fountain, Jane passed the open door to John's conference room. His voice carried into the hallway: *I want it noted that she took all the good hangers.* She let out a giggle and found herself mysteriously thirsty. One trip to the water fountain became two, then three, each path conveniently taking her past John's open door. During her fourth "hydration break", she caught another snippet:

Could we add a right of refusal to seating arrangements during joint attendance at children's events? Determined on an alternating schedule, with Husband in odd years, and Wife in even years?

Jane couldn't resist playing this game too, and hurried back to her attorney, already formulating her own ridiculous addition in her head: *Grocery shopping decisions shall be made independently by the parent during their respective parenting time, with no required accounting to the other parent.*

Fast forward eight hours. The agreement was finally done. Sixty-five pages of legal jargon, schedules, and divisions. It was time to execute the agreement. Jane's hand trembled slightly as she took the pen. Not from sadness. From holding back laughter. There it was. Page fifty-seven, Exhibit A, line fourteen: "couch cushions and couch mattress". Not "couch." Never caught. Never questioned. Her little rebellion preserved in legal language. The signing ceremony felt oddly formal. Each stroke of her pen felt like cutting another tie. Initial here. Date there. Full signature on this line.

Her attorney carried the papers away, disappeared down the hall to collect John's signatures.

The attorneys gathered the papers, collating them with practiced efficiency. Copies for everyone. It was done. Actually done. Jane felt a lightness she hadn't experienced in years. She couldn't help but grin: Not only was she done, but she was also free to laugh.

John's Journal: "Agreement secured. Maintained custody of the apartment and ninety percent of the furniture. She left with hand-me-down mirrors, a wobbly coffee table, a tiny rug, and a suspicious smile."

Jane's Journal: "The End :) "

Epilogue: In the annals of divorce court proceedings, Jane's story would be remembered as a reminder that sometimes, the sweetest victories arrive in the most ridiculous packaging—wrapped in toilet paper rolls, seasoned with "stolen" extra-virgin olive oil, served on half a couch. It wasn't about winning. It was about becoming whole again.

A couch split in two.

CURTAIN CALL

#MASHTHEAVOCADO

#Mashtheavocado

So, what's next? For both of our characters, a new chapter begins, one where joy, happiness, and, fingers crossed, sanity will rule. They will start fresh, hearts unburdened by the weight of what came before. As yesterday's storm is becoming smaller and smaller every day, they discover that happiness and beauty lie in the brave act of letting go.

Walking away can be an act of bravery. When you part ways with someone who no longer brings joy or nurtures your best self, you are not just ending a chapter; you are stepping into a future where your happiness and growth take center stage. Finally. It's about honoring your worth and recognizing that life is too precious to waste on anything less than fulfils you. Seek the joy you deserve now—not in fifteen years when your kids go to college, or fifty years when you find comfort in a nursing home with communal game rooms and a heated pool. Seek it now. In this very moment.

#MashTheAvocado if you are unhappy!

And throw a guacamole party with your friends afterward?

Jane soon realized that mashing the avocado wasn't just something you do once and move on. It was more like a daily practice. She'd smashed her way out of an unhappy marriage, but co-parenting meant the ingredients of her old life still mixed with the new one. The trick was maintaining her own flavor while sharing the spoon. Every time the kids switched houses, every text about early school pick-up or extra-curriculum activities—these were all chances to practice her mashing skills. Sometimes the mixture was chunky, sometimes smooth, but it was always authentically hers.

John and Jane's parenting schedule has become a finely choreographed routine, with kids hopping back and forth between homes and returning with a new collection of T-shirts, underwear, pants, socks, and other treasures that the other parent might be tempted to "borrow" (rather than sending the clothes back to their rightful owner, neatly packed in the kids' backpack). A few weeks into this domestic dance, an unexpected twist left Jane baffled: She received a love note from her ex-husband.

A love note! Can you imagine the awkwardness of the situation? The first love note appeared on Milo's socks where the word "DAD" was written in bold black marker and in capital letters. The socks, once dull and grey, now bore those three letters. She blinked, rubbed her eyes, then looked again. Yes, there it was—unmistakable. She held the sock up to the light like it was some ancient treasure she'd just discovered. What could it mean? "DAD", as in "Deeply Always Dedicated"? Jane was still pondering the secret meaning behind the love note when she started folding the kids' clothes after doing laundry. To her surprise, Mia's purple panty was also marked "DAD"! Same three letters, same mysterious love message! So this wasn't just one lost love note written in a moment of weakness; it was a strategic move. John has marked at least two items with his now-signature love note. Could it be? He wanted her to know he was still around. Could it be his attempt to revive their relationship? A regular black marker would have likely washed out in the laundry, but it seemed that John had used a fabric marker, designed to withstand the washing machine's turmoil. Perhaps, like a fresh coat of paint, it was his way of showing that his message, however subtle, wasn't going anywhere, even after the divorce cycle.

Jane scanned all her children's clothes, her heart racing as she hoped to uncover some clue that might explain this odd gesture. True to form, John had been meticulous—every shirt, every pair of pants, every sock he was keeping at his place was marked. The only item he could not mark was Mia's scrunchy. Jane figured that was just too small for a "DAD" endorsement.

Jane couldn't help but think about all the time and effort John must have put into this little outreach. How should she respond? All night long, Jane was going back and forth: Should she respond "MOM" ("Marvelous Original Move") on the clothes she bought for the kids and kept at her place? A simple "MOM" would be a nod to his creativity but nothing more, right? Or should she sever all ties once and for all? After much thought, Jane decided to let the gesture go unacknowledged, hoping John wouldn't be too heartbroken by her silence.

As our two strangers were settling into their new lives, punctuated by text messages coordinating their kids' schedules and unexpected love notes written in black marker, John and Jane independently ventured into the modern dating world. The online scene was completely new for them—after all, these two millennials had met long before dating apps became the norm. With a mix of curiosity and trepidation, they created their first profiles. After months of photographing their fridge contents, John and Jane had accidentally become experts at making the ordinary look appealing—a skill that came in surprisingly handy when choosing their flattering dating profile pictures.

Jane was both amused and amazed by the variety of profiles and personalities out there. All "available" at her fingertips. Depending on the apps, the options ranged from swiping right, left, or even up or down. And let's not forget the "Super Swipes," "Super Likes," or "Compliments," each promising to make her stand out—except, of course, she hadn't paid for the premium service. So naturally, none of her grand gestures would go through . . .

The whole experience was an emotional rollercoaster. And on some apps, matches came with a ticking clock—if she didn't make a move in time, the connection would vanish, leaving her wondering if she'd just let "the one" slip away into the digital abyss. Oh, the pressure of connecting to a stranger who could potentially change your life is palpable! Jane still remembers one particular match—he extended the connection by twenty-four hours. At first, she didn't even know that was a thing, so she Googled it. She could not believe it! He *paid* to extend the match! He paid to have a chance to meet *her*! She felt like she'd hit the jackpot, or at least won a mini lottery. Flattery level: off the charts. Then, came the timeless internal debate: *Do I play it cool or do a happy dance? Maybe both? Should I send him a rose? No wait, roses are for a different app. Can I cross-app? Not sure. How about an emoji then? But which one?* She was completely overwhelmed and realized she probably needed more than twenty-four hours to figure out the best response to this grand romantic gesture.

Soon, browsing through dating profiles became her (guilty) pleasure. Oh, the reading! The endless fodder for jokes and laughter! And oh, the pictures! Jane couldn't help but chuckle at the myriads of profile photos featuring furry cats or grown men posing with their mothers at family gatherings. Pictures labelled "as seen on my mom's fridge" were her favorite, as she realized her own photo collection could be captioned "As seen on my own fridge", though that probably wouldn't attract many matches.

What truly fascinated Jane, however, was decoding the mysterious language of dating profile interests. What did people in Boston claim to love?

Many potential suitors listed coffee. Jane initially assumed they were brewing their own as a hobby. Turns out they were just buying overpriced coffee from local trendy cafes. Jane wondered if she should list "avocado enthusiast" in her profile, then thought better of it. Some wounds were still too fresh, and explaining her complex relationship with the fruit might scare away potential matches. So, she listed "water" as her top interest. "I love water."

And then, there was "mindfulness" which always came with a brain emoji next to it. What even is that?

Jane thought, *My mind is full too, full of pictures of strangers I will never meet.*

But the real gem came when she saw someone list "aquarium" as an interest. Intrigued, she swiped. Was it right, left, up, down? She couldn't recall. And oh, delight, they matched. Immediately, she pictured their first date, her dressed head-to-toe as Nemo, nervous but excited. Had she taken the "aquarium enthusiast" thing too literally? Maybe. But his profile screamed "I love aquariums," so why not have a little fun? On the way to the date, Jane texted a friend: *I hope he appreciates the effort. I mean, these orange and white stripes took some serious dedication. Oh, and the fin on my back? A bit cumbersome, but it adds authenticity, right? I wonder if he will dress up too. Could you imagine if he shows up as a scuba diver? That would be hilarious.*

Okay, almost there. Deep breaths. Ready to dive into this date— literally and figuratively.

Whatever happens, at least it will be a story to tell.

ABOUT THE AUTHOR

Rose Ajar is the pen name behind the comic tale Who Ate the Avocados?

Rose is a millennial juggling a full-time job, a rarely-visited gym membership, a caffeine habit, an ever-growing laundry mountain, two lively kids and one very patient divorce attorney.

With her authentic style, sly humor, and a knack for turning chaos into comedy, Rose's writing offers a refreshing dose of laughter and perspective for anyone navigating the absurd rollercoaster of divorce—or just life in general.

If this book made you laugh, cry, or question your avocado consumption, **please leave a review—Rose can't wait to hear your thoughts!**

Printed in Dunstable, United Kingdom

76455218R00091